A KINGS MC ROMANCE

CASTLE OF
Kings

BETTY
SHREFFLER

Melissa,

Enjoy the wild ride !

♡ B. Shffl

CASTLE OF KINGS

Published by Betty Shreffler
Copyright © 2017 by Betty Shreffler

This is a work of fiction. Names, characters, places, and incidents are either the product of the author's imagination or are used fictitiously, and any resemblance to actual persons, living or dead, business establishments, events, or locales is entirely coincidental.

Printed in the USA.

ISBN: 978-0692977064

Editor: Sandy Ebel—Personal Touch Editing

Cover Design: Marisa Rose Robyn — Cover Me Darling

FROM THE AUTHOR

To be in the know for all my alpha bad boy releases:

--> Subscribe to my newsletter via my website at: bettyshreffler.wordpress.com

--> or also follow me on Amazon at: amazon.com/author/bettyshreffler

If you like kickass fun readers' groups, with hotties, jokes, guest author takeovers, book specials, giveaways, then come hang out with me in my Facebook readers' group; Betty's Beauties and Bad Boys, where I love to get to know readers and share sneak peeks into upcoming works!

If you'd like a personalized signed paperback or Author Betty Shreffler memorabilia visit my Website.

Now time to meet Jake Fucking Castle! Enjoy!

CHAPTER ONE

LIZ

AS I APPROACHED the aged, wood sided Kings' MC house, it felt as if the last four years hadn't changed a thing. Harleys lined the side of the street due to the overflowing parking lot. The sound of music and voices carried well beyond the walls, sending a sensation of nostalgia straight through me.

I glanced up at my brother, Nix, and took in his appearance. Four years had given him a few extra creases around his vibrant green eyes, but he's still as good-looking and fit as the last time I saw him. While I was away at nursing school, he kept up the bike shop and bar, helping to pay my tuition. If not for him, I wouldn't have been able to return home with my Bachelor's in Nursing.

Being completely out of touch with the current club members had my stomach fighting a slow swirl of nervous butterflies. My feet began to lag on my way up the steps.

"Why the hell did I agree to come here?"

Nix rested his hand on my shoulder and ushered me toward the entrance, a grin splitting his lips.

"It'll be fun," he assured me.

"You know I don't do your parties."

"Trust me, you'll have a good time. My brothers will be on their best behavior with you here. Besides, there's a couple of them I'd like you to meet. I could see you hitting it off."

"I must have been desperate to agree to this."

"Liz, you always think my brothers are wild misfits," Nix chuckled. "Well they are, but that's not all we are. There's so much more to the club and the men who belong to it."

"You mean beers, bikes, and women?" I snickered, turning to face him.

Nix's face twisted into a frown. "How about the charity rides and events?"

I let out a breath in self-resignation. "Fair enough. And what is the event tonight?"

"A charity auction *and* it's fight night."

"Fight night?"

"Yeah, you'll see later. The guys will place bids and whoever wins gets his choice of whatever he wants. Most take cash, some pick something out of the shop for their bikes, some have special requests. Whatever they want. That's the rules."

"This should be interesting."

As we reached the doors, a cacophony of voices, clinking glasses, and boots shuffling the floor mixed with the loud, heart-pumping music in the background. Nix pushed the doors open and placed his hand on my lower back, guiding me into the crowd. Familiar faces, wearing the usual black vests or jackets with the silver skull and crown, lifted from their conversations and waved at us.

Nix stopped at the first table and began his evening of playing host. Being naturally social and a man feared as much as he is revered, he fits the role perfectly. When our Uncle Dallas who'd practically raised us passed away, he left the bike shop and bar to Nix. Nix couldn't have been happier to take over. Nix was a spitting image of Dallas in every way—looks and personality. The discussion of whether or not Nix really was Dallas' kid had come up in conversation a few times among the club members, but that rumor was never proven. Our mother took off on us when we were kids, and we haven't seen her since. Our father died from cancer a couple years later, leaving his brother, Dallas, the responsibility of raising two rebellious pre-teens. To everyone's surprise, we turned out to be well-behaved human beings, most of the time.

"You look beautiful tonight," my Aunt May crooned in my ear. Meeting her gaze, I took in the longer length of her hair and the new gray streaks accenting her amber eyes. She twisted one of my long, loose, dark curls around her finger and flipped it off my shoulder. "Nix will have to keep a protective eye on you. Every man in here is going to want your attention."

"Well, Aunt May," I clicked my tongue against my cheek, "you know my attention is hard to get."

"That's my girl. Make those men work for that tail." With one swift slap, her hand came across my ass.

"You're too much." Shaking my head, I grinned at my spirited Aunt. I pointed toward the bar, getting Nix's attention. "I'm getting a drink."

He nodded and continued on with his meet and greets. Aunt May walked with me to the wood top bar, the Kings emblem mounted proudly on the wall behind it. I rested on the stool and smiled at the long-time bartender, Jeff.

"Two shots of blackberry bird dog and a beer to chase it down."

"On the house, Liz." He set the drinks on the counter and slid them toward us. "Nice to see you. It's been a while."

"Thanks, Jeff. It's good to see everyone."

Aunt May tapped my leg and raised her shot glass, waiting for me to take mine. I lifted it and clinked hers before tilting the glass to my lips.

"We missed you around here." Jeff set his elbows on the bar and leaned forward. "It's good to have your shining face back."

4

"She was too smart to stick around." Aunt May pushed her empty glass toward Jeff. "Went off and got herself an education. I'm proud of you, doll."

"Thanks May. I enjoyed nursing school, but I'm glad to be back home. It's not the same anywhere else."

"Of course not." Jeff picked up the empty shot glass and it disappeared under the counter. "This is where your family is. This is your home."

Lifting the beer from the counter, I swiveled my stool and looked over the crowd of club members and those who accompanied them.

"Yes, it is."

I'd grown up in this environment. A place where everyone looked out for each other and treated one another as family even if you weren't blood. I knew just about everyone in the room, save a few new members who'd joined while I was away. These people were my family and it was good to be home.

Across from the bar, a man walked in wearing a black, leather jacket with the familiar club patches and a worn-out ball cap. I couldn't see his face, but I noticed the way others reacted to him. Several women adjusted their cleavage before following him like lovesick puppy dogs. A group of guys by the pool table nodded their heads, and he moved in their direction, ignoring the women as if they didn't exist. They pouted their ruby red lips and slunk back to their tables.

Pointing my beer in his direction, I asked Aunt May who he was. She looked through the crowd to the man I was watching. He shimmied out of his jacket, and I couldn't stop watching the show. The lights over the pool table highlighted layers-upon-layers of rock hard muscles covered with black ink from wrists to shoulders. His chest stretched out the black tank he wore tucked into his dark, denim, ripped-up jeans and studded belt.

"That's Jake Castle. He joined the Kings shortly after you left."

"What's his story?"

"He's from Georgia, but somehow ended up here in Nashville. He became fast friends with Nix and Trevor. He became a member pretty quickly after that."

"Huh." I glanced at Nix who was still making his rounds. "I should bring Nix a beer. He can't seem to get away from his fans." I turned to Jeff. "Can I have another?" I asked, waving my beer at him.

With a pat to my leg, Aunt May returned my attention to her.

"Nix's done well while you were away. The Club has benefitted from his leadership. The shop and bar are doing good, and he's even built a relationship with local law enforcement. The Kings help keep an eye on things, you know, in places they can't."

"What about the other crew? The Wild Royals still around?"

"Unfortunately, yes. They opened a bar on the other side of town. They've been competition. The word is they're running drugs through the bar."

"Of course, they are. Wouldn't expect anything less of them. Correction, yes, I would."

Jeff brought the other beer, and I left Aunt May to take it to Nix. He gave me a profound thank you and wrapped his arm around me.

"Liz, I want you to meet Dillon," Nix nodded to a handsome guy with messy blond hair, blue eyes, and a large red and black tribal tattoo spiraling around his right arm.

"Nix says you just got back from nursing school. Congratulations."

"I did, thank you. It's good to be home."

"Are you staying for good?"

"Yeah, I've put in a few applications at the local hospitals. Hopefully, something will come of it."

"I'm gonna get the auction going. I'll get with you later, Liz."

Leaving me with Dillon made it clear he was one of the guys Nix hoped I'd *hit it off with*. So far, Nix wasn't wrong. Dillon was attractive with a deep voice and sexy Australian accent.

"Want another one before it gets crazy in here?" Dillon pointed to my nearly empty beer.

"Sure, thank you." I walked with Dillon to the bar and took the same stool as before while Dillon ordered us another couple of beers.

"Nix says you like to go riding."

"I do, yeah."

"Wanna go with me sometime?"

"I might," I cocked my head and grinned.

Dillon chuckled. "Nix warned me you wouldn't be easy to win over."

"Maybe you can coax me with dinner and a ride," I smiled behind my new bottle of beer.

"I'm definitely up for that. What do ya like to eat?"

"Italian."

"I know a place. How about tomorrow at seven?"

"You don't waste time, do ya, Aussie?"

"Not in a place like this, you don't," Dillon winked at me and gave a cheeky grin, "and not when a woman is as attractive as you are. There's gonna be guys lining up to ask you out."

"So far, you're at the front of this non-existent line."

Dillon's smile turned to a frown. I followed his eyes and turned my stool to see who he was looking at. The man with the ball cap and black tank top was standing next to me ordering a beer. He glanced at me and winked, then flashed a pearly white smile with dimples below dark, brown eyes on a face that would melt any woman's panties. I couldn't peel my eyes away from the ripped, tatted, towering hunk of muscle who was making me wet just looking at him.

"You Nix's sister?" He took his beer and leaned against the counter.

"Yeah, Liz."

"He didn't tell me you were gorgeous."

"Well, he didn't tell me anything about you, *at all*. Must have slipped his mind."

Jake let out a chuckle, and I watched his full, kissable lips pull back into a smile. Even his laugh was attractive.

"You gonna be here a while?"

"Probably all night."

"Good. I'll catch ya later, Peach."

"Peach?" I said to Jake's back as he walked away. He looked over his shoulder and winked at me, giving me that same ridiculously charming smile which sparked sexual yearning smack dab between my thighs.

Dillon touched my arm, and I looked over at him, feeling embarrassed I'd forgotten his existence.

"So, is tomorrow at seven good?"

"Oh, yes. Yeah, seven is good. You can pick me up here."

I smiled when I saw Nix approaching the bar. He put his arm around me and pulled me away from Dillon.

"I'll bring her back. I just need her a moment."

Nix guided me to the farthest corner of the room, away from listening ears and the music.

"What's up?" I asked, meeting his serious gaze.

"I see you met Jake."

"Yeah. Is he one of the others you thought I'd hit it off with?"

"No," Nix said coldly. "He's one of the ones I want you to stay away from. Jake's an asshole and a womanizer. I don't want you anywhere near him. Anyone, but him."

Hearing him say that with such passion, brought disappointment burrowing into my chest.

"All right. I'll steer clear of him. Dillon asked me out tomorrow night. Is that okay?"

Nix ran his hand through his lengthy, jet, black hair and let out a breath of relief.

"Yeah, Dillon is a nice guy, but still, don't let him try to take you home."

"Got it, Chief. When's the auction starting?"

"Now. Let's get a seat."

CHAPTER TWO

LIZ

AN HOUR LATER with everyone liquored up and carrying different possessions to their tables, I was doing my best not to notice Jake's watchful eye catching me across the room. When he started in my direction, I turned my stool toward the bar, putting my back towards him.

Solid, massive arms wrapped around each side of me, locking me between them. His lips grazed my ear as he whispered just for me to hear.

"You look lonely, Peach. I can remedy that."

I turned my stool to face him, still locked in his arms and only a few inches from his gorgeous face.

"Oh yeah, how's that?"

"Come home with me tonight."

This guy definitely had a set on him. Even with the immediate attraction to his sexy-as-hell body and his delicious cologne assaulting my senses, I wasn't going to make it easy for him.

"Lemme guess. You're used to women dropping their panties at your request?"

His lips pulled back into a devilish grin. Pressing his knee against mine, he spread my legs and moved between them.

"I'd like to watch you drop yours."

The scent of whiskey and beer lingered in the air as he licked his lips and waited for my response. The glimmer in his eye told me he was expecting me to say yes. He was used to getting what he wanted. Leaning forward, I grazed my lips against his ear. His hand went to my thigh, already sure he owned me.

"You're gonna have to try a lot harder than that, playboy." Placing my hand on his waist, I stepped off the stool and moved him backward. Surprise swept over his face, but a man like this doesn't give up easily.

His hand took hold of mine as I moved past him. With my hand in his, he abruptly turned my body to face him. With his free hand, he held me in place, locked against his body. He leaned down, brushing his scruff against my cheek.

"When you change your mind, I'm gonna enjoy watching those perfect little lips beg me to fuck you."

"You should find yourself a new toy to play with. I don't do one-night stands or cocky playboys." His arrogance was too much for just one man. I put my hand on his chest and scolded myself for enjoying the way he felt beneath it.

Just when I expected a new line to spill out of his mouth, he adjusted his hand and rubbed my back with his thumb.

"I like you, Peach. I want to get to know you. I can't do that here."

"What's with the nickname?" My brows pinched inward.

His hand raised my chin, bringing me closer to his lips. My body tingled, feeling needy for his touch. I knew this man's kiss would be phenomenal, but I had to control my wistful desires. Nix had warned me he was a womanizer, and so far, he'd proven to be just that.

"You look like you'd be just as sweet in my mouth."

I stared up at his bold, brown eyes looking down at me, pulling me deeper into his web and damn, if he didn't know he had me in his crosshairs. His lips parted into a grin.

"I think you'd like that, wouldn't you, Peach?"

I adjusted my footing as I grew wet under his penetrating stare. Movement around us pulled me from our heated tension. I glanced in Nix's direction and his dark, green eyes narrowed in on us.

Jake leaned into my ear as his thumb dipped into my jeans and gave my hip a tug, pulling me against the firm knot in his jeans.

"We'll continue this later."

He walked away from me, leaving me standing there with my breath heavy and an unwanted sexual yearning aching between my legs. I stepped up to the bar and ordered another shot. The smooth, warm liquid had just gone down when Nix approached. He placed his hand on my arm and gave it a squeeze.

"What'd he say to you?"

I glanced down at his hand. His grip was unusually tight. I removed his hand, he looked down, and his face reddened, realizing he'd left a mark.

"I'm sorry. I didn't mean to."

"I know you didn't. What's gotten into you?"

"Nothing, don't worry about it. The fight is gonna start soon. Stay close to me, okay?"

Club members were moving tables out of the way, clearing the area in the center. A few guys stripped down, removing their jackets, vests, or t-shirts. Money exchanged hands and bets were made. I caught sight of Jake moving through the crowd toward Nix. Holding several bills, he extended his hand.

Nix looked down at the money. "Who's it for?"

"Me," Jake responded coolly.

"You never fight. What changed?" Nix glared at him, eyes narrowing.

Jake glanced at me, looked back at Nix and deadpanned.

"Tonight, I have a reason to."

Nix snatched the money from Jake's hand and leaned toward him, saying something private, so I couldn't hear. Just as Nix finished whatever he had to say, Jake walked away with an arrogant smirk smearing his face. Nix's temper was on the verge of flaring. The vein in his temple was bulging, and his jaw was locked. I touched his arm, and his cold eyes softened when they looked at me.

"What was that about?"

"Nothing for you to worry about." Nix put his arm around my back. "Just some club business. You ready for this?"

"How bloody is it going to get?"

"Oh, c'mon you're a nurse, you should be used to seeing blood."

"Yeah, from accidents, not from people intentionally hitting each other's faces."

"It's good for the club morale, and we're men, we enjoy this shit." A deep rumble of laughter escaped Nix's chest.

Two men were already moving into the center. I recognized one of them as Wesley, one of the older members who ran with my Uncle Dallas. A younger man—tall, bald, with ink covering his back and traveling up his neck—raised his fists across from Wesley. One of the club members on the sideline held up his cell phone and a buzzer went off.

The younger guy with the neck tattoo lunged instantly, but Wesley raised his arm and blocked the fist aimed for his face. Wesley went low and slammed his fist into the younger guy's ribs. He buckled over, holding his side and immediately put space between him and Wesley. Wesley went in for another shot, but the younger guy twisted and turned his body. Wesley's arm swung through the air, and the younger guy took the advantage and put a left hook into Wesley's jaw. Wesley's eyes darkened. The man took the hit like a champ. No doubt he'd received a few in his years. With two more swings, Wesley had the younger man hunched over, spitting up blood. The buzzer sounded and money exchanged hands. Wesley had won that round.

This display of testosterone fueled fist-play continued for another round before it was Jake's turn. He stripped off his black tank and revealed an intricate puzzle of tattoos covering his shoulders, ribs, and lower back. Nix nudged me, and I checked to make sure I wasn't drooling. The man going up against Jake was Lucas, a long-standing member of the club and nearly as big as Jake. They eyed each other carefully, then Jake raised his boulder-like arms in the air.

The buzzer went off, Lucas took a step and swung. Jake leaned his body back and dodged Lucas' fist. Jake moved his feet, luring Lucas in a circle, seeming to study Lucas' body language. Irritation filled Lucas' eyes, and he swung, putting weight into his punch. Jake blocked the swing and slammed his own fist into Lucas' face. Lucas stumbled backward, and a few club members caught him, then tossed him back into the makeshift ring.

Lucas came at Jake again and clipped him in the jaw. Jake shook it off and landed a fist in Lucas' chest. Lucas stumbled back, the wind clearly knocked out of him. Jake paused, showing restraint, letting his opponent collect himself. Moments later, Lucas came at him again, and Jake grabbed his arm, locked it in place, quickly turned his body and flipped Lucas over his shoulder. Lucas landed on the floor and didn't bother to get up. The buzzer went off, and Jake reached down and gave Lucas his hand. Lucas stood, giving short, heaving breaths.

My nursing instincts kicked in and I headed toward Lucas. Nix grabbed my wrist and stopped me.

"Let him get out of the ring and to the side first. He doesn't need everyone to see you nursing him. It'll embarrass him."

I nodded, knowing Nix was right. These guys didn't like to show weakness, even when they were wounded. I walked around the outside of the crowd to where Lucas was sitting. Someone handed him a shot and he chugged it. With his face squinting, he tried to sit up straight.

I took the seat next to him and gave him a sympathetic smile. "It's been a long time, Lucas." He nodded and bit back a grimace. "Let me have a look at you." I lifted his shirt and saw the bruising already taking place. "You've got a broken or bruised rib. You'll need to rest and cough when you feel you need

17

to, even if it's painful. If you don't cough, you put yourself at risk of a chest infection."

"I need another damn shot is what I need." He touched his tender chest and grimaced.

"Listen to me," I frowned at him, "I know what I'm talking about."

"Yeah... Nix said you just... got back from nursing school."

"I did."

"Sorry... I didn't get a chance... to welcome you back."

"It's all right. I saw you were busy with the blonde. Where'd she go?"

"That's my girl, Crystal. She left... to go to work... night shift."

"Ah. Well she's a looker."

Lucas tried to laugh, but couldn't.

"Want another shot?"

He nodded.

"I'll get ya one, bud. Sit tight."

As I returned from the bar, the winner of tonight's fight night was being chosen. The three winners were put into the center, Nix raised each of their arms and the crowd cheered for each one. When they got to Jake the cheering escalated. Nix's disappointment was obvious. Jake took a bundle of money from Nix's hand, then pulled him in to say something. Nix leaned back and his eyes darkened. His stare was deadly; he was clearly pissed about whatever Jake had said.

Nix shook his head and the VP of the club, Pat, chimed in. Some kind of argument was happening between the three of them. Finally, Pat made a declaration and both Nix and Jake stopped arguing. Jake developed that same smirk I'd seen earlier when he'd spoken to Nix, and Nix looked as though he was ready to put fight night into another round.

Some of the crowd quieted down as I handed Lucas his shot.

"Jake has chosen what he wants," Pat spoke up over the remainder of the crowd.

Nix and Jake's eyes stayed locked on one another. Pat glanced at me and grinned, then spoke loud enough for everyone to hear.

"Jake has chosen Liz."

CHAPTER THREE

———

LIZ

STANDING OUTSIDE THE door of Nix's office, I could hear his fist hit the desk before he barked out in anger.

"Damn it, Pat, I should've seen this comin'! What the hell is he thinking claiming her like that? In front of the whole damn club?"

"He's ensuring he gets what he wants. You know he's a smart shit. What ya gonna do about it? The rules are the rules. Besides it's only one night, and Liz is a grown woman."

"It's not enough he fucks his way through every woman who enters the club, now he wants my sister too. She's not a fuck-and-dump he can do as he pleases with. I'm gonna make that shit clear right now!" Nix's heavy boots thudded toward the door and then stopped at the sound of Pat's voice.

"Don't do anything stupid, son. These rules are in place for a reason. Liz can take care of herself just fine."

Nix let out a huff and stormed out the door. I kept myself out of sight, against the wall, until he disappeared around the corner. Pat walked out, and I stepped forward, catching his attention.

"What's going on between Jake and Nix? There's more to it than what he's telling me. He's far too angry."

"Been there the whole time, ain't ya?" A smile stretched across Pat's face. "You did the same when you was a kid, too. I remember Dallas catching you countless times and tellin' ya not to listen in on the men's business. Well nothin's changed, darlin'. Let Nix handle his business."

"Don't treat me like a child just because I don't have a dick, Pat." Looking him in the eyes, I squared my shoulders. "You should know better by now. I don't take orders from anyone."

Pissed off and done with the drama for the night, I headed back to the front room to say goodbye to my Aunt May and to tell Dillon I'd see him tomorrow. I entered the bar to find Jake, Dillon, and my brother having a heated conversation of their own. Forget it, the date with Dillon wasn't important enough to interrupt that conversation. I hugged my Aunt May goodbye and waved to a few others I'd caught up with throughout the evening.

Several eyes followed me around the room and watched me walk toward the exit of the bar. Someone whistled behind me and I glanced back to see someone nodding their head to Jake and my brother, alerting them I was leaving.

Jake started towards me and Nix grabbed his arm. With a menacing stare and a few words spoken, Jake stayed back, and Nix came after me. Nearing my car, I could hear Nix's boots pounding the ground behind me.

"We need to talk," Nix said as I opened my car door.

"About what?"

"That date with Dillon isn't going to happen."

"Why?" I crossed my arms, my anger already surging through me.

"Jake will be coming by tomorrow to pick you up instead."

His comment took me by surprise. I admit I was attracted to Jake, but I'd seen what Nix had warned me about. Jake was a cocky playboy, and I wasn't interested in having any part of that.

"I thought you didn't want me anywhere near him?"

"What I want doesn't matter. He won the fight. He chose you. There's nothing else to talk about. He'll be coming over tomorrow at seven to pick you up. You'll need to be ready. After the date, you can tell him to piss off, but you're gonna have to go on the date."

"Jesus, Nix. I'm not some damn kid or puppy you can arrange play dates for."

"I don't want this anymore than you do, but the rules are the rules."

"I don't belong to your Club. I don't have to follow any rules."

"Damn it, Liz, you're a part of this family as much as I am. Don't make this any harder on me. Go on the damn date, then tell Jake to go fuck himself."

"Fine, but you'll owe me, and you know I'll collect."

"You've made things a lot easier on me by doing this," Nix ran his hand through his hair and let out a breath, "and yeah, I'll owe you big, cuz I have no doubt Jake's gonna be a pain in the ass to deal with. And don't give into his games neither."

"Anything else?"

Nix turned back toward the entrance of the bar.

"Yeah, don't dress sexy."

It was ten minutes before Jake was supposed to be picking me up for our date, and I was still scrambling to get ready. I put on my dark liner, a fresh coat of gloss, and slid my black, leather skinny jeans into my black boots. My gray t-shirt had cursive script-like writing on it that said, *Not For Sale*. I couldn't help feeling like the shirt was appropriate for a date with

23

Jake Castle. One last glance in the mirror at my long, dark, loose curls and smoky green eyes, and I was ready to go. I tucked my wallet in my back pocket and headed downstairs. Nix came waltzing in the front door of our home, a beer in hand.

"What are you doing over here? I thought you were workin'?"

"I came to check on you."

"Really? I can handle a date." I grabbed my leather jacket and slid it on.

Nix looked me up and down and frowned.

"You look too good."

"Get over it. I'm not changing."

"Be careful tonight."

"Jeez, you act like I'm going out with a criminal. Wait, am I? Does he have a record?"

Nix shook his head. "He's clean. nothing more than speeding tickets and a disorderly conduct which was dropped."

"All right. Anything else I need to know?" I was hoping he'd share whatever it was which seemed to be stewing between the two of them.

"Nothing. Have a good time, but don't let 'em in your pants."

"I got the chastity belt on and threw away the key," I laughed and gave him a reassuring smile. "Nothing to worry about."

The rumble of a Harley vibrated the walls as it pulled up to our house. My stomach churned with excitement. The thrill of a new ride always did get me buzzed and whatever he was driving sounded like it could satisfy.

I patted Nix on the shoulder and said my goodbye. He stood at the door and watched me approach Jake's bike like a father watching his daughter go on her first date. He was even equipped with an expression mixed between disappointment and fear. Jake didn't seem to notice Nix's presence. He watched me walk to his bike, then laughed and shook his head.

"What's so funny?"

"Nice shirt," he said, handing me his helmet.

"Thought you'd like that."

I clipped the chin piece as I slid on behind him. After tucking my arms around his waist, I glanced back at Nix who'd disappeared inside.

"Where we headed?"

"Somewhere private."

The rumble of his Harley vibrated my body as he started it up and pulled out of the drive.

Soon we were moving through traffic, making our way to the strip downtown. The dark evening made the lights of the city a beautiful dome of scenery as we drove through. Jake stopped at a light, and as we waited, he rested his hand on my leg. The warmth of his touch felt good on a cool night like this. As the light turned green he caressed my leg, then took hold of the handle, taking us off down the rest of the strip.

Just outside of the main strip, he pulled off to the side of the road and parked. I unclipped my helmet and looked up at the restaurant sign. We were standing outside of a hole-in-the-wall Italian restaurant I loved.

"How'd you know?" I smiled at Jake, surprised by the gesture.

"Your Aunt May."

"Nicely done, playboy." The guy sure did have game. No doubt he did recon before every date.

A smile stretched across his face as he took the helmet from me and set it on his bike. Walking up to the restaurant, his hand fell to my lower back, holding me close to him and guiding me to the door. To my surprise, he outstretched his arm and opened the door for me.

The podium at the front said, *Seat Yourself*, like it always did. I pointed to a booth and slid into the seat, tossing my jacket in the corner. Jake slid right into the same side, trapping me between him and the wall. I laughed and tried to nudge him down the seat, but his massive frame didn't budge. He glanced over at me and smirked, then grabbed the side of my ass and tugged me toward him. His arm stretched around me and settled on the back of the seat. He leaned close and grazed his scruff across my cheek. His breath tickled my ear, sending a shiver over my body.

"I like you close to me, Peach. Get used to it."

He leaned back and raised his hand, placing his thumb on my lower lip and pressed it down. I could see the hunger fill his eyes. He leaned in, ready to replace his finger with his tongue, but the waitress disrupted that plan.

"Welcome to Illano's. What would you like to drink?"

After the waitress walked away, Jake turned to me. I couldn't help feeling like every time he looked at me he was hypnotizing me. His stare was sensuous and dangerous and I found myself wondering what it would be like to be kissed by him. Then I reminded myself of how many women had no doubt fallen for those warm, chocolate eyes and enticing smile.

"What should I order?" His words were smooth as silk, slipping out of perfect, full lips and coated with masculinity. He licked his bottom lip and waited for me to answer. Watching him study me told me he was intelligent. The wheels were always turning in this man's head. I'd have to be on top of my game to dodge his smooth moves, or I'd end up as putty in his hands.

"What do you like?" I asked him.

"That's a loaded question. I like a lot of things." The sexual connotation was clear. Was everything about sex with him?

"Go with the lasagna." I closed my menu and pulled my delivered drink close, sipping while looking at anything but those chocolate eyes. The waitress returned and took our order, and I went back to looking at everything else, but him.

His warm hand slid in between my thighs and gently squeezed my leg. Surprised, I turned my head sharply and glared at him.

"Thought that might get your attention," his grin widened. "I brought you to your favorite place, but you don't seem to be enjoying yourself. I'm not that bad to be around, am I?"

"No, Jake," I laughed at the dejection in his voice, "you're not terrible to be around, but I'm not looking to be another notch on your belt either. I agreed to this date, that's it, then you and I will go our separate ways. There's plenty of other women who come to the club for you to toy with."

"That's what you think?" His jaw ticked as he removed his hand. "That you're a new toy?"

"Pretty much, yes."

"Well I'm not gonna lie. I'd like to see this,"— he tilted his head toward my body—"naked in my bed, but I have no intention of tonight being the only night we see each other."

"Hmm, well that's unfortunate for you because that's exactly my plan."

"We'll see about that," the corners of Jake's mouth creased.

Dinner came and Jake praised me for my choice in food. He even kept up the conversation and had me laughing uncontrollably. When dessert was offered, he said yes and ordered us strawberry covered cheesecake. When it came, he shocked me by taking the fork, cutting a sliver, and bringing it to my mouth.

The fork slid from my lips, and he watched me with the same hungry eyes I'd seen earlier. His hand slid between my thighs and this time, I didn't jump. He leaned in and put his warm breath to my ear. His hand slid up higher and kneaded my inner thigh.

"I want you to come home with me. Say you will." His lips pulled my ear between his teeth.

"I can't." Arousal coursed through my veins like hot oil. My head was dizzy with lust.

"But you want to."

I glanced up at the fierce want in his eyes and moved his hand from my legs before I lost total control of my sanity.

"Even if I do, it's not happening."

Jake smirked at me before grabbing the check and leaving the table to pay. Immediately, I missed the warmth and presence of his body. I grabbed my jacket and headed to the restroom. After collecting my wits, I walked outside to find him leaning against his bike, his legs outstretched, crossed at his feet. He looked delicious sitting there on his motorcycle, black leather jacket and a sexy-as-hell smile. As I approached, he handed me his helmet.

"You ready for the next place?"

"Next place?" I laughed. "Sure, as long as it's not *your* place."

He glanced back, the corner of his mouth raised. I hopped on and he drove us to a bar on the strip.

When I got off, he wrapped his arm around my back and guided me inside. As we walked to the bar, his hand slid into the pocket of my jeans and stayed there as he ordered us drinks.

"I'm not just a toy, huh?"

"You're better than that." His gaze swept over me, capturing me and locking me with his heated stare.

"You're right. I am." Pride tickled my belly, but the reminder of Nix's warning quickly stomped it out. "You wasted your prize."

"I don't think so."

"Is that why you brought me here to the bar? A few drinks aren't going to change my mind."

The heat in his eyes didn't help the scorching need between my legs. Constantly battling my desire was becoming torture. As if he sensed it, his hand on my ass tightened and with one swift movement, he pulled me to him and kissed me. The kiss was sudden, unexpected, and my body responded instantly. His mouth was a mixture of soft lips and hard, dominating need. I couldn't get enough of him, and he clearly felt the same. His hands tightened on my waist, pinning me to him as his lips continued to ravage me.

The bartender slid our drinks toward us, making a sound to get Jake's attention. He growled into my mouth and looked at the bartender like he wanted to come across the counter and pummel him for interrupting. Jake picked up the shot and swallowed quickly. I did the same, still reeling from the kiss. Jake motioned for another two shots, then looked down at me, studying me closely. His penetrating eyes had taken my emotions captive. My body and mind were lost in this moment. He took hold of my hip and pulled me back to him, raising my chin, pressing his thumb into my lip.

"You do something to me, Peach." His thumb dipped into my mouth and I claimed it, sucking the tip. He stared down at me with dangerous secrets in his eyes. Secrets of what he wanted to do to me, secrets I was dying to know. Taking his hand off my waist, he wound my hair around his hand and tugged.

"Tell me, what do I do to you?" My head tilted up to him, my lips parted.

"This is what you do to me." He took hold of my hand and placed it over the tight knot in his jeans. He rubbed my hand over him while still watching my reaction. "We should get out of here."

Jake downed the second shot and paid the bill. His palm stayed glued to my ass as we walked out of the bar to his motorcycle. He reached for the helmet, then clipped it under my chin. He got on, waited for me to get comfortable, then tightened my hands around his waist, glancing back at me before starting the engine.

The smell of his cologne and the warmth of his body taunted me the entire ride out of the city. As the lights of downtown faded into the distance, the reminder of Nix's words came back to my mind. I was doing exactly what Nix told me not to. I was falling for Jake's games and was probably less than an hour away from being another notch on his belt, another club girl he'd use and toss aside without remorse. When we stopped at the next light, I leaned in for him to hear me.

"I need to go home tonight. I can't stay with you."

He didn't say anything, but I knew he understood when he took the turn that led to my house. After pulling into my drive and cutting the engine, he got off and took the helmet from my outstretched hand.

I didn't know why, but a heavy weight pressed against my chest. I was a fool for feeling it, but I felt guilty making him take me home.

"I had a better time than I expected." I couldn't read him. Whether he was upset, felt nothing, or was confused, I didn't know, his face showed no emotion.

"Good night, Jake. I'll see ya around."

As I turned to walk away, he took hold of my wrist and pulled me back to him. His lips pressed into mine, rough and greedy, pulling my lust back to the surface, dampening every part of me. When he let go of me, my body nearly fell back into him. He caught me, looked down at me, and brushed his thumb across my cheek before turning back toward his bike.

"Good night, Peach. I'll see you tomorrow."

CHAPTER FOUR

——

LIZ

THE NEXT DAY was a rough one. I hadn't slept well after leaving our date. The tossing and turning didn't help me with my interview at the Nashville Medical Center. After the interview, I stopped by Nix's office to give him a briefing on the night before. I hadn't seen him since I left for our date and knew he'd be anxious for the details.

With it being lunchtime the bar was quiet with only a couple members and a small group of customers drinking and playing pool. As I approached Nix's office, I heard Pat inside with him. I put my back against the wall and listened.

"Can you believe this shit? Now they want us to make a deal with the Wild Royals. Don't they know it doesn't work like that? We're rivals. We can't step foot in their territory without guns blazing."

"Of course, they know. They don't care. They expect us to come up with something. I say we do it.

Bring in a third party. Pay them to buy from the Wild Royals. See if the agency will give us marked bills."

"It's too risky, and if the Royals found out, we'd be seen as traitors."

"Think about it, Nix. It's a hell of a chance to eliminate them. We owe them for what they did to Bear and May."

"Don't share any of this with the brothers until I have time to think about it."

I hurried down the hall at the sound of them leaving their chairs. By the time Nix reached the bar, I was sitting there with a drink in hand.

"What are ya doing here?"

I turned my stool toward him as he took the one next to me. "I came to tell ya about the date."

"And?" Nix rubbed his thumb over the other like he always did when he was nervous.

"I didn't sleep with him. We had dinner and drinks, then I asked him to take me home."

Nix's arm reached out and took hold of my neck, pulling me closer, so he could kiss me on my forehead.

"I'm proud of you." As he stepped off the stool, he turned his head toward me. "Why don't you come back tonight. There's a party. Dillon will be here. You can reschedule your date now that the deal with Jake is over."

"I'll think about it. Before you take off, I want to talk to you."

"About what?" Nix turned back to me with concern in his eyes.

"Let's go in your office."

Nix rested his feet on his desk and leaned back in his worn-out office chair as I settled into the seat across from him.

"So, what's the need for secrecy? Spill it."

"I overheard you and Pat. I didn't like what I heard."

"You shouldn't be listening in on our business."

"It wasn't intentional. I came to speak with you and overheard."

"Uh huh, I know you better than that. Besides, I don't want you worrying about the Club's or my business. I'm a man, Liz. I can take care of myself, and I'll do what I think is best. You know that."

"Getting involved with the Wild Royals is dangerous, and you know it."

Nix's eyes wandered off toward the window facing the woods and our house, just down the street. "This isn't open for discussion." His gaze fell back on me. "Don't tell anyone what you heard in here and don't ask questions about it either." Nix's phone rang and he pulled it from his pocket and looked at the screen. "I gotta take this. It's a supplier. I'll see you later?"

"Yeah, I'll make an appearance. This conversation isn't over though."

Nix smirked before answering his call.

I walked back to our two-story, white siding, ranch home and climbed into the shower. The hot, soothing water eased some of the worry and tension I had building in my neck and shoulders. It seemed Nix was considering the deal with whatever investigative agency he was working with. The thought of it terrified me. The Wild Royals were outlaws and unpredictable. The consequences of dealing with them could be detrimental to everyone involved.

Once out, I wrapped the towel around me and headed toward the closet for something fresh and casual to wear. I pulled the string of the light bulb and started sorting through my clothes. The old hardwood floor creaked behind me, and I jumped at the sight of the delicious man standing in the closet doorway, holding the frame as he leaned in and looked at me, a smirk smearing his face. His hungry eyes did a slow burn up my legs, to the towel, then lingered on my breasts before settling on my face.

"Don't leave the front door unlocked anymore. I don't want a man sneaking up on you like I just did."

"*Why* are you here, Jake?"

"Get dressed and meet me downstairs. I'm taking you out."

"No, and you have no right barging into my house and waltzing into my bedroom. What if I was naked?"

"I would've been one lucky bastard." Jake leaned his weight against the frame of the door. A devilish grin stretched across his face. "If only I'd arrived a few seconds later."

"You're impossible." I let out a frustrated breath. "Get out of my room."

"See you downstairs." He turned and headed toward my bedroom door.

When I walked into the living room, Jake was sitting on my dark emerald couch with his legs spread, his elbows on his knees, a beer in his hand. His black t-shirt revealed the intricate ink designs along his arms. Part of me wanted to have a closer look and discover every detail of his artwork. I squashed those thoughts immediately when a flutter of butterflies did a loop in my stomach.

"I see you've made yourself comfortable."

He raised his head and his eyes landed on me beneath his worn out, tore up, black ball cap.

"You look good."

"Yeah, I'm really working it in my jeans, tank, and ponytail."

Jake set the beer on the glass end table and stood to his full six-foot height. At five-foot-four, I had to look up into his warm, chocolate eyes. His hand reached up and thumbed my lip, a habit I noticed he was developing.

"I think you'd look good in anything, but even better with nothing on."

I stepped closer and placed my hands on his hips as I spoke just within reach of him kissing me.

"You'd really like that, wouldn't you?"

His hand took hold of my ass and squeezed it as he pulled me against him.

"You already know I would."

Before I could say another word, his mouth crashed into mine, bringing my lust surging to the surface. His tongue invaded my mouth with wanton need and his firm hands held me steady as he palmed my ass and fisted my hair and neck in his other hand. His kisses were like little tastes of fire on my lips, burning straight through to the core of me that yearned to have every sexual desire sated.

His hand moved up, his fingers finding their way beneath my shirt. His warm, firm grip pulled me toward him, locking me against him, so I could feel his arousal pressing into me.

His lips left mine, and I remained there in a daze, trying to regain logic and control the burning lust aching between my legs.

"Let's go upstairs."

Those three words snapped me right out of my daze. I slid out of his arms and headed toward the door.

"Goodbye, Jake."

I opened the car door to my old, red Camaro, not looking back at him. I pulled out of my driveway as quickly as I could and took off toward the restaurant where I was meeting my friends.

While sitting at the booth in the restaurant, I couldn't shake a nagging feeling. I wanted more than Jake's kiss, but I refused to be just another club girl he'd toss aside when he was done playing.

"Liz."

My head snapped back toward Jenna's perky voice.

"Sorry, I was lost in my thoughts."

"Yeah, you were. So, what time is the party tonight? It sounds fun." Jenna's big, brown, doe eyes locked on mine, obviously eager for details.

"It's at seven-thirty. There'll be lots of cute guys. I'm glad you both wanna come. It's not fun going by myself."

"Of course, we'll come." Ashley swung her long arms around me. "We're so happy you're back. We missed you." Her long, blond hair fell over her shoulders onto mine.

"I missed you guys too." I flicked her hair out of my face and gave her a peck on the cheek. "It's been too long since we got to do something together."

"Now that you're back we'll have to make up for lost time." Jenna wiggled in her seat. "I'm thinking girl's night—slumber party at your house."

"You just want another chance to kiss Nix." Ashley looked at Jenna and smirked.

"Oh my God," Jenna's large, brown eyes widened, "shut up, that was years ago. We were teenagers."

"You liked it, J," I laughed at the fake traumatic look on her face. "Don't deny it. You'd totally pucker up if he wanted to kiss you again."

"He's gonna be at the party tonight, right?" Jenna bit her lip and grinned as her cheeks took on a rosy hue.

"Of course, he is. He's the President of the Club now."

"That is really hot." Jenna fanned herself. She let out a breath and scrunched her face. "Why does your brother have to be so sexy?"

My sweat tea nearly came out my nose as I laughed.

Ashley giggled next to me, then turned her head toward me. "What about you, Liz? Did you meet anyone at school?"

"Yeah, I did, but it didn't work out."

"Why not?" Ashley asked, jutting out her bottom lip.

"He wasn't, I don't know—"

"Bad boy enough for you?" Jenna finished.

"Ok, yes, he was a little too clean cut for me. After growing up with a bunch of tough badasses, I can't help it. He didn't own a motorcycle, and you know that's pretty much a deal breaker for me."

"When you gonna get your own?" Jenna asked.

"Don't really want one of my own, I want a man who will take me riding on his. There's a guy I'm interested in who'll be there tonight. His name's Dillon. Has an Australian accent."

Jenna and Ashley's eyes widened.

"Yum! Can't wait to meet him," Ashley said.

"You'll get to tonight."

CHAPTER FIVE

LIZ

AFTER SETTING Ashley and Jenna's bags in my room and some extra fussing over hair and makeup, the three of us headed to the Kings MC house. As soon as we walked into the bar, my eyes instantly scanned the club members for Jake. My nerves settled when I didn't find him. Maybe I'd get lucky, and he wouldn't come tonight. Jenna's hand took my arm, and she let out a quiet squeal.

"There's Nix. I'm gonna go talk to him."

Ashley and I looked at one another and giggled.

"We'll have a shot waiting for you at the bar," I called out.

"Uh huh," Her voice trailed off as she maneuvered through the busy tables to where Nix was sitting. She flung her red curls off her shoulder, and to Ashley and I, that meant she was about to put on the charm.

"Your brother doesn't know what's coming, or does he?"

"He's oblivious," I laughed and shook my head, "has no idea she has a crush on him."

"Pity, they'd be really cute together."

"I know, right? I'd be happy to have Jenna as a sister-in-law."

Ashley and I moved in step with one another toward the bar. We settled on the stools and chatted up Jeff while he made us drinks. After a toast and tossing back the shots, Ashley's eyes scanned the club members.

"Where's this Dillon guy?"

"He's the dirty blond playing poker." I looked around and found him sitting at the table next to Nix with several other club members. "The one with the tattoo wrapping around his arm." Just as I pointed his direction, he looked up at me, the corner of his mouth raising as he nodded at me.

"He's a hottie."

"Not bad, right?"

"Oh yeah, he's totally your type."

"I think I'll take him a beer."

"Good move."

I turned to Jeff and ordered two beers. I gave Ashley a wink as I headed to the table where Dillon was sitting. As I came up behind him, I reached around and set the beer down next to his nearly empty one, showing no emotion at the four of a kind he held in his hand.

"Nice hand," I leaned in and whispered.

He winked at me and patted his leg. I slid in, and he wrapped his arm around me, resting his hand on my thigh. Throughout several games, money exchanged hands and our flirting increased. His hand moved farther up my thigh, then settled on my hip and ass. He pulled me tighter to him, completely losing interest in the game altogether.

"Why don't you two take it upstairs," Max barked.

"Let's go up to the bar," Dillon whispered in my ear. "They're serious players here."

Dillon took my hand and led me to the bar. As we neared, my smile left my face. Jake was standing next to Ashley with his hand affectionately on her arm, yet his eyes were locked on me. I'd been so distracted by Dillon, I never saw him arrive at the club. His eyes traveled to Dillon holding my hand, then narrowed, before looking back at Ashley. He said something funny, and she laughed, moving closer toward him. Jealousy erupted, wreaking havoc on my emotions. Dillon didn't seem to notice. He pulled me up to the bar and wrapped his arm around my waist as he ordered us more drinks.

"Liz."

I heard Ashley's voice calling my name; I dreaded looking her direction. My hand swiped the shot from Jeff, and I swallowed it quickly before looking.

She waved, indicating she was leaving and mouthed, "I'm gonna go." Jake deadpanned in my direction, put his hand on her back and guided her through the crowd. I stood there in shock, angry that earlier in the day he was kissing me, and now, he was taking my friend home to have sex with her. Relief washed over me that I hadn't fallen for his games. I could see how easily I would've been tossed aside.

Suddenly, Dillon's presence wasn't enough of a distraction. I tried to keep up conversation, but my mind kept wandering off, thinking about Jake and Ashley and what was surely going on between them. I was pissed and yet, had no right to be. I'd turned Jake down twice, and I hadn't even mentioned Jake to Ashley, but the jealousy was still digging a deep hole in my chest.

Dillon must have noticed the change in my mood. He told me he wanted to get back into another poker game and abandoned me moments later. I sat at the bar alone, upset, and ready to go home.

"Why so glum, buttercup?" Jenna found me and patted me on the back.

"You having fun?" I asked. Her cheeriness was not something I was in the mood for.

"Yeah, but you don't look like you are. What happened to the cute blond you were hanging out with?"

"He went back to playing poker. I wasn't fun company."

"I'm actually getting somewhere with Nix. You mind if we stay a while longer?"

"Yeah, sure." My mood instantly went from foul to worse.

I wasn't about to make nice and chat with anyone with my bad mood. I preferred to be alone to brood over how shitty my night was going. After ordering a couple more beers, I took them with me to the back porch, behind Nix's office. I dragged a chair close to the railing and rested my legs on it as I sat back and drank my foul mood away.

Twenty minutes later, the liquor and beer hit me, and I rushed past the front room to the bathroom. On the way back, I noticed Jenna still sitting at the table with Nix, looking like she was having a great time. Seeing that only stirred my irritation further. I was way past ready to go home, but wasn't about to ruin her night. I ambled back to the porch and leaned down to grab my empty beers. Footsteps behind me had me turning quickly to see who was joining me.

"What do you want?"

Jake had his knee bent, and his back and boot against the wall.

"How much have you had to drink?"

"What do you care?"

"Why are you mad? Did Dillon upset you?"

"It's not your problem, Jake. Why are you back anyway? Ashley wasn't enough for you? Or did she bore you, and you're looking for more entertainment?"

"You're upset I left with her?"

47

"No! You can do whatever you want. I just don't get you. Earlier today you were kissing me in my living room, and a few hours later, you're taking my friend home to have sex with."

"You're jealous." A wicked smile spread his lips.

"I'm not jealous," I huffed and rolled my eyes.

"You seemed happy with Dillon. Why get upset over me leaving with Ashley?"

"Really?" Hearing her name escape his lips put my anger into overdrive. "You need to ask? I was flirting with Dillon. You had *sex* with Ashley."

"Did I?"

"You did, didn't you?"

"What if I did?"

"Enough with the games, Jake. I'm not in the mood." I stormed past him, and he stretched out his arm, catching me by the waist. With ease, he pulled me into his arms. His warm chocolate eyes looked down at me, and I saw that same hunger fill them before he kissed me.

"Seriously!" I raised my hand to his chest and shoved him back. "You just had sex with my friend and now, you're trying to kiss me. Fuck off, Jake. Stay away from me."

"You've had too much to drink." His hand took hold of my wrist, pulling me back to him.

"Jake, my patience is wearing thin. Let go."

"Calm down." His grip tightened and he turned my body toward the wall, pinning me between him and it.

"I'm not going to calm down. You're an asshole, and I want you to stay away from me."

"Fine, but you need to be taken home."

"It's not gonna be you," I spat.

"Damn it, Peach."

My back went to the wall and his lips slammed into mine. I pulled my head back and slapped my palm across his cheek. His hand took hold of my wrist.

"I didn't have sex with her."

"What?"

He let go of my wrist.

"Why not?"

"Does it matter?"

"Yes."

Jake's eyes narrowed in on mine. "Seeing you with Dillon, I didn't like it. I want you all to myself, but if you pull a stunt like that again, I'll do more than just give your friend a ride home."

My jaw dropped, and I struggled to form words in my drunken state. His hands slipped into mine and raised my arms above my head and brought his lips within a whisper of mine. His bold, brown eyes studied my face.

"I don't play nice. I'm not a nice guy."

His kiss came quick and fierce, ravaging my mouth and claiming it with his. He left my lips and covered my neck, leaving a trail of wet kisses up then back down. My head leaned back as my body betrayed me, arching forward, wanting him to touch me, wanting his mouth and hands to claim every part of me.

"But I don't think you want a nice guy. Do you, Peach?" His hot breath seared my ear, sending sparks igniting throughout my body.

"I don't."

"You want me, don't you?"

He released my hands and took hold of my waist as his lips came back to mine. His tongue ventured in and out, making my breaths heavy and leaving me aching for more of him. His hand caressed my hip before both hands unbuttoned my jeans. Every frustrated feeling—between my brother's warnings and my shit storm of confused emotions—evaporated the moment his fingers touched me. My head tilted back, and I moaned with relief.

"Fuck, Peach. You're soaking wet for me," he growled into my mouth as he claimed it with an aggressive need, teetering me over the edge. He added another finger and pressed against my clit, working me into a frenzy as I gyrated my hips against his hand and moaned with pleasure.

"Tell me what you want, Peach. Say it, so I can hear you."

"Make me come, Jake. Please, make me come."

"That's what I wanna hear."

His mouth went to my neck and in between wet kisses, he'd bite and nibble, then kiss softly again, his fingers working me into a rag doll sagging against the wall. I wrapped my arms around him for support as my knees grew weak, moaning through my orgasm.

His arm held the wall next to me as he leaned in intimately. "I like the way you sound when you come in my hand, Peach. I wanna hear it again, but only next time, louder." His kiss came soft and affectionate. He removed his hand and took me by the waist, holding me close to him. "I'm taking you home with me. There's no way in hell I'm leaving you alone, drunk, and eager to have a cock in you."

CHAPTER SIX

LIZ

JAKE RUBBED MY thigh when he cut the engine outside his small ranch home.

"Check your phone, Peach."

After removing his helmet, I pulled my cell from my pocket and glanced at the screen. I'd been worried before we even left the bar about leaving Jenna behind. She'd responded with lots of emojis and thanked me for leaving her with Nix, who'd given her a ride home on his bike.

I let out a breath of relief, and Jake chuckled at me before taking my hand, leading me to his front door. On the other side of his door there were sounds of excited whimpers and claws scratching on a crate. Jake opened his door and set his helmet on a black, metal stand below a wall mount with pegs for jackets. On the other side of his bachelor pad living room was a boxer puppy eagerly waiting to be let out. Jake opened the crate and the large puppy nearly tripped over its giant feet to get to me. When he went to jump, Jake scolded him and the puppy sat down, its tail bouncing on the floor, waiting for attention.

"I can't believe it. Hard ass Jake has a puppy."

The corner of his mouth raised. "His name's Rocky. Ten-month-old boxer."

I scratched behind Rocky's ear and his leg started tapping the floor.

"You got 'em trained already?"

"Of course. No dog of mine is gonna be unruly." Jake whistled, Rocky snapped to action, and followed Jake to a back door. They disappeared outside, and I walked around Jake's house, checking out everything in sight. He had a small, brown leather couch sitting in the center of the living room with an aged, heavy, metal chest as a coffee table. In front of that was a TV stand made of some kind of thick, quality wood with a large screen TV above it.

Straight ahead was a kitchen with fairly new appliances and an island with bar stools which cut right through the center. Behind the kitchen was a mud room with the door to go out back. To the right of the kitchen, a hallway led to a bedroom and bathroom on the left side and another smaller bedroom on the right. Jake's bedroom was clean with dark, wood furniture, and a large, black and white framed photo of a Harley motorcycle on the wall.

Looking at the nightstand beside the bed had me wondering what I'd find inside. A box of condoms was my first guess. I slipped into his room and turned on the lamp. My hand was on the knob of the drawer when I heard the backdoor open. I clicked the lamp off, rushed out of the room, and back down the hall. Jake put Rocky back in his crate, then watched me as he shed his jacket and tossed it on the island. He leered at me with a mischievous grin before he turned and stalked toward me. I giggled at the provocative look in his eyes and sprinted toward his bedroom.

Within a few steps, he had me locked in his arms. His heated breath warmed my ear.

"You like the chase as much as I do, don't you, Peach?" Fingertips trailed across my abdomen as he pulled my ear between his teeth. His hand dipped into my jeans and rubbed me until I was wet with need.

"Yes, I do," I breathed.

His left hand took hold of my breast and kneaded it in his hand as his fingers dove deeper, his hot searing kisses leaving imprints on my neck.

"I want you to undress for me. I wanna see everything."

"What makes you think I will?" His skilled hand already had me weak in the knees.

"Because you want to." His finger pulsed against my clit and my breath escaped me.

When his hand left me and he sat, facing me on the bed, I nearly pounced onto his lap and stripped us both, but when his eyes fell on me, the obvious anticipation and arousal made my body buzz with excitement. I wanted to give him exactly what he wanted because he was right, I wanted it too. Jake reached over and clicked the lamp on as I slowly lifted my shirt over my head. Leaning down with my ass in the air, I untied the strings to my boots and slid out of them. Next came one bra strap, then the other before unclasping it and letting it fall to the floor.

Jake ran his hand across his chin and licked his lips as his eyes stayed locked on my body, watching every movement with that predatory look he had every time I was in his sights.

Slowly, I unbuttoned my jeans and slid them over my hips, revealing the matching black lace thong. He bit into his bottom lip, his eyes resting on the V-shape of my underwear. With my thumbs hooked onto the straps, I pulled them off and let them drop to the floor before stepping out of them.

Jake rose from his bed and placed his hands on my hips, slowly tracing them over the curves of my frame. With those dark, brown eyes fixated on me, he palmed my ass and lifted my legs, wrapping them around his waist. He turned me toward the bed and laid me on it.

"Moan as loud as you want to. I wanna hear you unravel beneath me."

One hand took hold of the outside of my thigh as his head went down to my waist. Slowly, his tongue flicked across my belly button, then left a wet trail down to the dampest part of me. When his mouth claimed me, my back arched. I could barely contain the euphoric sensation coursing through me, and I hadn't even reached my orgasm. His wicked tongue dove and resurfaced and caressed over my clit only to repeat. My palms fisted his comforter as I moaned and begged for more. I was losing myself to this man's control and didn't want it to end. His fingers filled me, pussy and ass, and worked me into a trembling, moaning fanatic until I finally unraveled.

His lips gave soft kisses along the inside of my thigh, then continued up my stomach until he was laying on top of me. His erection pressed into me, and I raised my hips, putting him in the most pleasurable position. Taking hold of my thigh, he locked me against him as he pushed into me.

"Can you feel that? How much I want to bury myself in you right now?" His thrust came harder and I let out a breath of pleasure when the hard knot in jeans rubbed against my clit.

"Yes," I whimpered.

"Do you want me inside of you?" His lips moved against mine. He thrust again and I tilted my head back riding the wave of pleasure drifting through my body.

"Jake... please."

A sound of satisfaction escaped his lips. The pressure of his erection left me and was followed by the sound of his belt coming undone. Palming the fabric of his shirt, I hastily helped him remove it. His shirt swam through the air, his mouth slamming down on mine.

One hand wrapped around my hair tie and pulled it loose. Dark spirals fell around the palms of his hands. Instantly, he fisted the loose strands as his lips continued to ravage me.

Pounding at the front door, followed by the broken voice of a woman calling Jake's name, snapped me out of my joyride. Jake growled into my mouth, clearly irritated by the interruption.

"Stay here," he told me as he stepped off the bed. With his back to me, I could see his muscles had tensed. With one quick glance back at me, he adjusted his jeans and disappeared around the door.

The sound of Rocky's wagging tail hitting the crate was followed by Jake opening his front door. I dressed as quickly as I could and stepped into the hallway to listen. The woman was distressed and begging Jake to help her. Between tears, she apologized for not having anywhere else to go. As quietly as I could, I moved to the end of the hallway to see her. Jake's back was to me, his arms around the woman, soothing her and whispering something in her ear. She looked up at me, and I saw the damage around her eye.

"I'm sorry... I didn't know you had someone here."

Jake looked over his shoulder at me. His expression changed from one of affection to irritation. Embarrassed, I turned back toward his bedroom to get my shoes and leave as soon as possible. I finished lacing my second boot when he walked in.

"Don't leave."

"Who is she?"

"A friend."

"The kind of friend you have sex with?"

"Doesn't matter, it's in the past. I need to leave for a little while. I'm taking her to the Club, so she has a safe place for the night. I want you here when I get back."

"I think it's best I go home." I stood up from his bed. "Whatever that is," I pointed toward the woman in his living room, "doesn't look like it's in the past. There was something there. I saw it." I tried to move past him, but he took hold of my arm and pulled me to him. One arm wrapped around my lower back, the other held my face in his palm.

"I won't be gone long. Stay here... for me."

His eyes had gone soft. It was clearly important to him I stay. That shattered the wall I had built seeing him embrace the woman in his living room. A part of me wanted to walk out and not look back, but I knew I'd have regrets if I did. The emotion in his eyes was a magnet, pulling at my heart, keeping me in place, my curiosity on the edge. I nodded, and he raised my chin and gave me an affectionate, slow kiss.

"Anything you need, use it. I'll be back as soon as I can."

Jake's thumb caressed my cheek, then his warmth left me. I watched him walk out of the room and remained there until I heard the front door close.

CHAPTER SEVEN

——

JAKE

OUTSIDE MY HOUSE, my muscles tensed as my boots pounded the ground on the way to my Harley. "Where's he at?"

Behind me, Angela's footsteps hurried to catch up. "Don't worry about it."

"Apparently you do want me to worry about it," I stopped walking toward my bike and locked my eyes on Angela's, "or you wouldn't have showed up at my house."

"Jake, I'm sorry. I didn't mean to ruin your night. You were the only one I could think of who would help and not turn me away."

As the tears started down her cheeks, I turned toward my bike. I stopped being a sucker for tears years ago, and Angela was too accustomed to using them to her advantage.

"Tell me where he's at."

"He's a Wild Royal. You can't take that on, Jake."

I handed her my helmet and nodded for her to get on. "If you want my help, tell me where's he at." Straddling the bike, I waited for her to climb on and take hold of my waist. I glanced back waiting for her response. My ride wasn't going anywhere until she told me where the piece of shit who tore up her face was.

"He went to Spitzer's, outside of town."

"He alone or with his brothers?"

"I don't know. He might have a couple of them with him."

My boot hit the clutch, and I fired her up. I drove Angela to the Kings Club. The party had died out, save for a couple stragglers too drunk to notice anything unusual about me walking in with her. I kept Angela out of their sight and led her upstairs to one of the offices turned sleeping quarters.

"I'm gonna have to tell Nix you're here."

"Please don't." Angela's eyes widened and she let out a whimper. "I can be out of here before he comes in. I just need a place to crash for tonight until Rex cools off. I'll call a friend to come get me in the morning."

My eyes narrowed in on hers. "That friend better not be your ol' man, cuz he's not gonna be able to ride when I'm done with him."

"Don't, Jake. He didn't mean it."

"That's what they all say." My jawed tightened. I turned my back to her and walked out. Her black and blue face was plenty enough reason for me to hunt the bastard down. I hopped on my bike and headed to Spitzer's. When I rolled up to the bar, I assumed he was still there when I saw a couple of Harleys sitting outside. I looked at my watch, it was one-fifty-seven a.m. The bar would be closing at two.

I leaned against my bike and waited for the coward to come out. His drunken ass came walking out six minutes later with his arm draped around a woman dressed like a one-night-stand. His buddy came out behind him, stumbling with a beer in one hand and the other groping the woman Rex had his arm around. Their intentions with her were evident. Too bad for them I was about to ruin it.

"You Rex?"

The man's dark eyes lifted to mine. Annoyance and curiosity filled them. "Who the fuck wants to know?"

"Who I am doesn't matter, but the name of the woman you beat like a punching bag does."

He raised his chin. "How the fuck do you know Angela?"

"Old friend."

Rex removed his arm from around the woman and squared his shoulders. Just like I hoped, he wanted a fight. "You fucking my ol' lady?"

A smirk lifted the corner of my mouth. Being an asshole and a drunk was too easy to antagonize. "No, but I used to."

His arm came swinging and I quickly moved off my bike and dodged his fist. His movements were quicker than I expected. Repeated drinking had turned him into a functioning alcoholic. His buddy decided to jump in on the fun, only his ass was too far gone for a good fight. I slammed my fist into his face and he dropped to the ground like a sack of potatoes.

The click of a knife whipped my attention back to Rex. It was too late. The blade was already slicing through my t-shirt, splitting my skin in two. A dull ache and wetness filled the area. The scent of copper reached my nostrils when the blade came at my face. I grabbed his hand and used it as leverage to turn his arm and shove it down until his shoulder was twisting out of the socket, then slammed the side of my palm down on his elbow with the intention of breaking it. He bellowed and writhed beneath me. The woman started screaming at me that she was going to call the police.

"If you're gonna do it, get to it."

I buried my fist into Rex's face and blood spattered onto the sidewalk from his busted lip and probably broken teeth. My fist gripped Rex's shirt and jacket and dragged him toward me, so I could look him in the eye.

"I don't like fuckers who get off on hitting women. Be grateful I didn't kill you. Hit Angela again and next time, I will."

Before shoving him to the ground, I rammed my fist into his face, giving him the same black eye he gave

Angela. He fell to the ground, and I kicked the blade down the sidewalk, out of his reach. I looked up at the woman whose eyes were wide with a mixture of shock and terror.

"Need me to call you a cab?"

She slowly shook her head. "I drove myself."

"All right then." I turned my back on her, still high on adrenaline, and needing the road under my wheels to cool me down. After climbing on my bike, I glanced over at the woman and was relieved to see her getting in a car parked outside the bar. I waited until she pulled out, then did the same.

The adrenaline dump took its toll on the way back to my house. The relentless throbbing reminded me of the cut in my side. Blood had soaked into my shirt and jeans and the skin on my knuckles were busted open and covered in dried blood.

Pulling into my drive, Liz was the first thing on my mind. I hoped she wouldn't freak when she saw me. Her trust of me was already thin, but if she ever truly wanted to be with me, she'd have to learn I was impulsive.

When I walked in the door, all the lights were out. With only the bit of moonlight streaming through the living room window, I went to Rocky's crate and soothed his whimpers, so he wouldn't wake Liz who I assumed was sleeping. I walked to my bedroom and sure enough, she was lying in my bed, wrapped under the blanket, sound asleep. Seeing her lying there in my bed, waiting for me filled me with more satisfaction than I expected.

Needing to patch up my knife wound, I went into the bathroom and stripped down to my briefs. After cleaning out the wound and dousing it in alcohol, I covered it up with gauze and tape. I cleaned up my knuckles and face, took a few aspirins, then returned to my room. When I raised the blanket, my cock jumped at the sight of Liz in her thong and one of my t-shirts. Her ass was perfectly round and had enough curve I could squeeze her cheeks firmly in my hands. Damn, if I didn't want to wake her and finish what we started. The throbbing wound in my side reminded me it would have to wait. I slid in behind her, wrapping my arm around her.

She mumbled in her sleep, and the sound of her sweet and sleepy voice coming out of those full, pink lips had the hard shit around my heart crumbling. I pulled her body into my chest, resting my hand on the softest part of her, right between her thighs. She let out a drowsy moan and nuzzled her ass into my cock before falling fast sleep. I kissed her neck, then let sleep roll in once my head hit the pillow.

CHAPTER EIGHT

———

LIZ

I WOKE TO the warmth of Jake's heavy arm caging me against his body. I lifted his hand and noticed his busted knuckles. I turned in his arms to get a look at him, but his face was fine. He looked peaceful and content and as sexy asleep as he was awake. I ran my hand over his shoulders and chest, admiring his puzzle of tattoos. My eyes caught something bright white. Looking down, I saw the bandage. I immediately shook him awake.

"Jake, what happened to you? Were you in a fight?"

His eyes opened slowly and he grinned as he looked me in the eyes. "You sound worried."

"I am. What happened to you?"

His hand went to my waist and raised his t-shirt out of the way, so he could run his hands along my stomach before dipping his hand inside my thong. His fingers gently caressed up and back down, slipping me into a daze.

"Jake," I whimpered, before placing my hand over his, stopping him. "What happened?"

He inched toward me, putting his hand around my waist, pulling me the rest of the way toward him. "Let's talk about it later." He took hold of my hand, sliding it inside his briefs. He was rock hard and clearly eager for release. My curiosity got the best of me. I placed my hand around his shaft, shocked by the full length and width of it.

"I'm pretty sure you're required to register this kind of weapon."

The corner of his mouth raised into a sexy, mischievous grin. "I'm past registering. It's fully loaded, and I'm ready to use it."

I laughed so hard my sides began to hurt. Jake laughed too, then stopped when his side caused him obvious pain.

"Maybe not as ready as you think you are." I glanced down and saw blood had begun to soak through the bandage. "Let me look at it."

He laid back and put his arms behind his head, giving me complete access to his wound. I pulled back the bandage to find a knife had split him open several inches.

"You need stitches to close this up."

"Can you do it?"

I looked at him, surprised. "Yes, but I don't have the tools. You need to see a doctor."

"I have what you need."

I gathered the alcohol and fresh bandages while Jake dug a box out of his cabinet filled with surgical thread, a curved needle, holder, and forceps.

"Should I be concerned you have surgical tools on hand like a first aid kit?"

Jake shrugged. "It's easier to have my own." Without explanation, he walked out of the bathroom and into his bedroom. I followed him, setting the alcohol and bandages on the night stand next to the stitching tools.

"Got any numbing cream?"

"Don't need it." Jake laid back and put his arms behind his head again.

"Of course, you don't." Apparently, this wasn't his first time getting stitches. After cleaning his wound, I got the needle and thread ready and began the first stitch. I glanced at Jake to make sure I wasn't hurting him. He laid there without flinching.

"You gonna tell me how this happened and who that woman was?"

"You probably won't let it go if I don't, will you?"

"You're figuring me out already."

As I waited for him to share the information he didn't want to, I noticed several scars on his torso. They were easily missed when your eyes were drawn to his tattoos. It was concerning how many scars he had, but I couldn't bring myself to ask about something so personal.

"There's thirteen of them."

"What?"

"Thirteen scars."

My stomach knotted. He'd noticed me looking at them.

"My father was an abusive alcoholic. Would beat on my mom regularly. When I was about eleven, I started defending her, taking the hits, so she didn't. He didn't like his son getting in his way, so he tied me to a chair and cut me eleven times—one for each year of my birth he said. My mother managed to get a call out to 911. If she hadn't, I probably wouldn't be alive."

I stopped suturing his wound as my body went numb. "What happened to him?"

"He went to prison."

"And the other two scars?"

"Both were fights. One was a broken bottle, the other a knife."

Holding the needle holder and forceps in my hands, I stared at him, still absorbing what he'd just shared.

"I've never told another woman how I got the scars."

"Why'd you tell me?"

"Last night, I left a man with broken bones because of what he did to the woman you saw in my living room."

"That's how you got this?"

He nodded.

I looked back down at his wound and finished the last few sutures.

"And the woman from last night, she means something to you?" I swallowed the lump in my throat and waited for him to answer.

"A little more than I normally care for a woman."

"Did you love her?" I stared down at the stitches, focusing on the last knot, avoiding his eyes. There was a pause and my chest tightened.

"No."

A surprising amount of relief filled me. Not that there was anything wrong with Jake having loved her, but a selfish part of me wanted to know what it was like to be the only woman to have Jake's love.

"I need to clean these." I set the tools back in the box.

Jake's gaze followed me out of the room. I could feel his eyes burning my ass cheeks peeking out beneath his t-shirt. As I sanitized the tools in the bathroom, he walked past and seconds later, I heard him letting Rocky out of his crate, followed by large paws smacking the floor, then the back door opened and closed.

I went back into the bedroom after putting the box away to check my phone. Nerves bunched in my gut when I saw a list of text messages from Nix. Each text was angrier than the last. I immediately dialed him.

"What's going on? Why are you blowing up my phone?"

"Are you with Jake?" His tone was cross and disapproving.

"I am."

"Have him bring you to the club. Now!" Nix hung up on me without an explanation. I hurried to get dressed and met Jake in the kitchen. Rocky ran to me and sat down, wagging his tail with trembling enthusiasm. I patted his head and scratched along his ear, making his leg kick like it did the night before.

"I just spoke with Nix. He wants you to bring me to the club. He's angry about something."

"We'll get there when we do." Jake stretched his arm and rubbed the back of his head as he let out a sigh. "I want you taken care of first. You hungry?"

"I am, but we shouldn't keep him waiting."

Jake opened the refrigerator and pulled out orange juice. After opening the lid, he chugged for several seconds before closing the jug and placing it back in the fridge.

"Whatever your brother is pissed about isn't going away. It'd be better if he has time to cool off. Take a shower. I'll get us something."

There was no point in arguing, Jake's expression had deadpanned. I'd have to leave on my own, and I knew that'd only upset him.

"I'm gonna smell like whatever body wash you got in the shower. Hope you like it."

71

"I want more than just the scent of my body wash on you." The corner of his mouth raised.

I couldn't help smiling at that innuendo as I walked to his bathroom.

I heard his bike rumble outside several minutes later. By the time I was out of the shower, dressed, and done using his toothpaste and my finger to scrub my teeth, he pulled up the drive. The smell of sausage wafted through the house as he entered. I joined him at the island and stood on my tippy toes to see what was in the bag. My stomach was growling, and I was appreciative he'd made me eat before going to see Nix. He wrapped one arm around me, pulling me close to his side. He leaned down and kissed me on the temple.

"You did good patching me up. I didn't thank you earlier and I should have."

Looking up at him while he dug containers out of the bag with one hand and held me with the other was causing my affection for him to grow. "Thank you for breakfast."

His hand wound through the loose strands of my hair, then caressed my back.

"Let's eat."

Jake had gone to a local hole in the wall diner. I knew the place. They made the best pancakes, and apparently, Jake knew that too. He'd ordered some for both of us.

"Can I give him a piece?" I looked down at Rocky's puppy dog eyes watching me eat my sausage.

Jake chuckled. "No, Peach. Don't spoil him."

"Aww, but Jake, look at those eyes."

"I like the way you sound when you beg me, Peach," Jake rubbed his hand along my thigh and eyed me with his masculine authority, "but the answer is still no."

"Fine." I jutted my bottom lip out at him.

A smile spread his lips. "You like him?"

"Yes, he's adorable and so well behaved."

"He likes you too." Jake squeezed my thigh before grabbing his empty container and tossing it into the trash. "You about ready to find out what got stuck up Nix's ass?"

I let out a breath. "I think I already know."

Jake folded his arms and leaned against the fridge waiting for me to explain.

"He told me to stay away from you. I didn't come home last night, then told him I was with you. He's obviously pissed about it."

"That why you didn't come home with me the first night?"

"It's not the only reason."

"Nix told you to stay away from me?"

Apprehensively, I nodded.

Jake looked off in thought, his face emotionless. "Let's go."

73

Twenty minutes later, we pulled up to the Kings Clubhouse. A couple motorcycles were outside, including Nix's; my stomach tightened. Was Nix going to threaten Jake to stay away from me? Was he being overly protective or was there something between them neither one was telling me? Part of me didn't want to walk into the club. I felt a storm was brewing, and I was the eye of the storm.

I climbed off Jake's bike and sat his helmet on the back. Jake took hold of my arm, pulling me onto his lap. His hand gripped my hip and the other wrapped around me as his lips pressed into mine. His tongue slipped in, coaxing our morning arousal back to the surface. The hand on my hip gradually moved between my thighs and caressed me, making me wet with need.

"I want you back in my bed tonight." His skilled hand stroked harder. "You tasted sweet, Peach, but I need more than just a taste."

As much as I wanted the same, I wasn't about to go against my own brother without knowing more details. I placed my hand over his to stop him before I lost all of my senses.

"Let's see what's going on."

Jake licked his lips; I could see his jaw tense. He eased me off his lap and stepped off his bike. We walked to the entrance, his hand rested on my lower back, and he opened the door for me to enter. When I walked in I saw a couple familiar faces playing pool, and Jeff was behind the bar, stocking fresh liquor for later in the day.

"Jeff, where's Nix?"

Jeff looked at Jake and I together, then motioned his hand toward the offices. "I'll let him know you're here."

Jeff didn't need to go far. As he turned the corner he almost ran smack into Nix's giant frame. I sucked in a breath when I saw the same woman from last night following him out. Nix's face was flushed, his eyes stone cold. He stared Jake down as he stalked toward us like a predator about to unleash.

"Damn it, she didn't leave," I heard Jake say aloud.

Jake pushed me behind him as Nix approached. The pounding of Nix's boots didn't slow. Nix swung and his fist landed on Jake's face. Jake raised himself and stared Nix down. I had a feeling the only reason he wasn't tearing into my brother was because I was standing there.

"Nix, what the hell has gotten into you?" I screamed.

Nix's eyes remained locked on Jake as if I didn't exist. "Stay the fuck away from my sister. You don't need to seduce Liz, too. She's not something for you to amuse yourself with."

"Jake, what's he talking about?"

"Of course, you didn't tell her," Nix huffed.

"What the hell is going on?" I demanded.

The other club members were approaching at that point. Jake spat blood from his busted lip and continued to stare at Nix, using what seemed like every ounce of his self-control not to retaliate.

"Ladies, go upstairs," Max said as he and Trevor joined us.

"No! I want to know what the hell is going on?"

"Go upstairs, Peach," Jake said without looking at me. His tone brooked no argument.

"Fine. Come on," I said to the woman behind Nix. She walked with me, and I guided her to the back porch of the Clubhouse. On the way down the hall, I heard their voices raise and scuffling back in the front room, then the sound of grunts and someone being slammed into a table. I didn't bother going back. I knew what was happening. They were fighting out their problems.

"We're not staying here. Our house is down the road," I pointed toward it. "I'm not gonna stick around and deal with their over-fueled testosterone."

"You're Nix's little sister, Liz?" she asked as she followed me across the yard.

I glanced back at the voluptuous redhead. Even with the black and blue marks surrounding her big, brown eyes and the scrape across her chin, you could see her face was pretty.

"Yeah. What's your name?"

"I'm Angela." She looked at me with surprise in her eyes.

"Should I know you?"

"No, I guess not." Disappointment swept across her face. "I'm sorry about last night. I didn't mean to show up unannounced. You Jake's ol' lady?"

I laughed at the term. I'd always thought it sounded ridiculous unless you were a biker's wife and over the age of forty-five. "No, I'm not his ol' lady."

"You his girl?"

The question lingered in the air. I didn't know how to answer. I honestly didn't know what I was to Jake.

"I'm sorry. I'm being nosy. It's really none of my business." Angela must have noticed the uncomfortable silence after her question. I glanced back at her and gave a half-smile.

"You're right. It's not."

We reached our house, and I opened the door, motioning for her to come in.

"I'm guessing all your stuff is at the home of the asshole who did that to your face?"

She glanced back at me with embarrassment in her eyes. She nodded.

"I have clothes upstairs you can borrow. You can use the shower too. After that, we can go to the store to get you some of your own things."

"You don't have to do that."

"You got anyone you can call?"

She shook her head. Tears were pooling in her eyes.

"Then, yes, that's what we're gonna do. Come on," I motioned upstairs, "my room is up here."

I walked to my closet and picked out a few different options for her. She chose an all-black outfit, creating an even edgier look than my own style.

"Thanks for letting me borrow these. I'll be quick in the shower."

"No problem."

I found myself fresh clothes, then texted Ashley and Jenna to see if they wanted to come shopping too. After getting them on board, I waited for Angela to finish. The realization hadn't left me that I'd been helping Jake's ex for the last hour. Thankfully, my goodwill was beating out my jealousy because she wasn't just Jakes' ex, she was a woman first and foremost, one who needed help. She'd obviously fallen for the wrong kind of guy and paid the price for it.

After the blow dryer ran for a few minutes, she stepped out, looking killer in my clothes. The jealousy did a somersault in my stomach, and I had to knock it back down.

"You wanna borrow some concealer?" I asked her.

"If that's all right?"

I helped her cover the bruises the best I could. It was barely noticeable now unless you knew what you were looking at. She smiled at me; I got a good look at how pretty she was. It was no wonder Jake was attracted to her. Her body was built like mine, but she was a little shorter which made her curves a bit more voluptuous. My breasts couldn't compare—hers were much larger and she clearly liked to put those puppies out there. She chose a low-cut shirt of mine which displayed them well. With her fiery red hair and my get up, she'd easily have a new man by the end of the day. I placed the makeup bag back in the drawer.

"You ready?"

"Yeah."

When we approached my car, Angela looked surprised. "This yours?"

I nodded. "'69 Camaro. It was my uncle's; he left it to me and Nix rebuilt the engine. I'm a fan of American muscle, man and machine."

"No wonder Jake has the hots for you," she laughed as she opened the door and slid in.

I didn't smile at the statement. I didn't want her to know how much I truly did enjoy hearing that.

"We're gonna pick up a couple friends of mine, then head to the drugstore and the mall."

CHAPTER NINE

—

LIZ

WE STOPPED AT a diner for a late lunch after shopping. Angela and Ashley took off to the bathroom, and Jenna scooted closer, so only I would hear her.

"What's the deal with this Angela chick? And what happened to you last night? You went home with one of the club members, right?"

"Ugh, Jenna. I'm in a mess. I went home with Jake Castle."

"Oh my God! I saw him! He's really hot. So, did ya?" She elbowed my side and winked.

"No, we got interrupted... by her." I pointed toward Angela's vacant seat.

"What do you mean?" Jenna's brows pinched inward.

"She's his ex-girlfriend, I think. Or ex fuck-buddy. I don't know. Either way, there was something between them. She needed his help last night, so he took off in the middle of the night to help her, but asked me to stay and wait for him."

"And you did?"

I nodded.

"Why?"

"I don't know. It seemed important to him I be there when he got back. He says whatever was between them is in the past. He called her a friend, a friend who needed his help. Nix lost it when he found out I stayed the night with Jake. They got in a fight about it this morning. There's something going on between them that neither one is telling me."

"Well, I don't like this chick. She seems like trouble."

"You sure it's not a little competition jealousy?" I flicked one of her loose, red curls. "Nix likes redheads."

"I know." The corner of Jenna's mouth twisted. "I want him to like *this* redhead, not *that* redhead," she pointed toward Angela coming out of the bathroom, but low enough Angela couldn't see.

"When we get back to my house, I'll talk to Nix and figure out where to take her. She must have family or a friend somewhere."

"Nix said the members are going to be hanging out at the club again tonight. You mind if we go?"

"Of course, we can." A smirk lifted my lips as I glanced at Jenna and winked. "I can tell how much you like him. I'll do what I can to help."

"Love you, sister." Jenna leaned over and kissed my cheek.

After the waitress took our order, Jenna set her eyes on Angela.

"So, where you from?"

Angela's eyes studied Jenna with displeasure before catching my gaze and changing her expression. "I'm from Jersey."

"How'd you end up in Nashville?"

"Followed an ex-boyfriend."

It was obvious Angela didn't want to play Jenna's twenty questions game, but she kept catching my watchful eye and answering each one.

"How'd you meet the Kings?" Ashley asked, chiming in.

"My ex was prospecting for them for a while before he left town," Angela's tone softened when responding to Ashley.

"That's how you met Jake?" I asked, swallowing the lump in my throat.

Angela glanced at me and gave me a half-smile as she nodded. Thankfully, the waitress brought our plates and ended the awkward tension.

Jenna and Ashley rattled off a few more questions, and I noticed the more they tried to dig, the more uncomfortable Angela got. She avoided any conversation about Jake or the Kings. I assumed it was to make things less awkward for me. After lunch, everyone piled into my Camaro and I dropped Jenna and Ashley off at Jenna's.

"I'll see you both tonight. Stop by my house. We can walk over together."

Once the both of them were out of the car, Angela and I rode in uncomfortable silence for several minutes before she spoke up.

"Your friends are nice." Her unenthusiastic tone told me they weren't her kind of friends.

"They are nice friends, but I could tell you weren't comfortable. I'm getting the impression you like to live on the edge. My first hint was you were dating an asshole, then the clothes, then trying hard to bite your tongue all day. You can be real with me. I'll respect you more if you are."

"I like the no bullshit directness," Angela let out a humored breath. "You're my kinda girl, Liz, but buttercup and dandelion are a little too sweet for me. I don't hang with chicks often. I'm a run-on-my-own kinda girl."

Finally, the real Angela was coming out, the spitfire I knew was bubbling under the surface, anxiously awaiting freedom.

"You seem street smart. How'd you end up with the asshole who marked up your face?"

"Same as you." Her smoky, shadow-covered eyes slanted at me. "I like 'em tall, tatted, and rough around the edges."

Hearing the words escape her lips like that had sirens going off inside my head. I didn't trust this woman at all. She may have been the battered victim last night, but how much of the tears were to get a reaction out of Jake? The woman I'd spent the day with today wasn't showing any residual effects of trauma. She seemed all too calm, cool, and collected. My curiosity about what happened between her and the boyfriend who hit her was eating at me, gnawing sharp little teeth right into my chest, but personal topics were clearly off the table between us.

"Any plans of where you're headed next?"

"I was thinking of sticking around for a while, spending some time with the Kings." A sly grin raised her lips.

With my stomach twisted into a knot, I turned into the driveway of our house. Nix's and Jake's bikes were parked side-by-side in the driveway.

When I approached the door, I heard them arguing. I walked in and they both went silent. Their eyes drifted back and forth between me and Angela.

"You two are still fighting? I thought you would have worked it out by now?" Irritated, I shifted my weight on my right heel and crossed my arms.

"You been with her all day?" Nix asked.

"Yeah." I glanced at Angela who seemed amused.

Jake's heavy feet pounded the floor right toward me. The swelling on his upper lip had gone down, but Nix had added a bruise across his jaw.

"Come on, Peach. We're leaving."

Nix's face was flushed and his eyes were stabbing darts into Jake's back. Their fight had left him with battle wounds too. He had a gash on his cheek, the surrounding skin still red and puffy.

"Don't go with him, Liz. We need to talk."

Jake took my hand and pulled me toward the door. I dug my feet into the floor and stopped him.

"I'm not going anywhere until one of you starts telling me what the hell is going on."

I looked from Jake to Nix to Angela who was leaning casually against the wall with an expression of levity I found odd.

"If I'd known, I wouldn't have let you leave with Angela." Nix stepped forward and ran his hand through his hair. "She's not someone I want you around."

"We need to go." Jake's arm wrapped around me.

Nervous tension built in my chest. I ignored him and returned my gaze to Nix.

"Why wouldn't you want me around her?"

"She used to be my girl until I walked in on Jake fucking her."

I slid out of Jake's arm and stepped away from him as anger swarmed in my gut. My eyes went to Jake first and his expression deadpanned, he wouldn't even look me in the eye. I looked at Angela and she shrugged her shoulder, as if to say, *it is what it is*.

"Get out. Take Angela with you."

Jake lifted his hat and rubbed the back of his head. "Fuck, listen to me, Peach."

"Get out!"

Jake glanced at Angela and nodded his head toward the door. She followed behind him.

I closed the door once they were out and glared at Nix.

"Next time you better damn well tell me what I need to know before I go and develop feelings." I stormed past him to the stairs.

"Liz!" The sound of heavy boots followed me up the steps. "I'm sorry. Liz!"

I stopped just inside my door. He stood on the outside with his hand on the door, keeping me from slamming it in his face.

"Had I known she was back, I would have told you. I never expected to see her again. She took off after the breakup, and I haven't seen her since."

"Why didn't you kick him out of the club? He broke one of the biggest codes and your trust."

"If I kicked him out, I would have to tell everyone why I was bringing it to vote. I'd have to admit that a brother was sleeping with my girl without me knowing. How does that make me look, as the

President, to not know my own woman is cheating behind my back?"

I opened the door wider.

"You understand why I didn't tell you now?" Nix gave me his bright, green, puppy dog eyes. "I was tore up about the whole situation. At least with her gone, Jake and I were able to be civil until he decided he wanted to seduce you too. That crossed the line for me. I blew up. I'm sorry I involved you like that. I did warn you about Jake, but you didn't listen."

"I thought I saw something in him, but clearly, I was wrong."

CHAPTER TEN

———

LIZ

THE NIGHT I kicked Jake and Angela out of our house I didn't attend the party at the club. I wanted to lie low and avoid Jake as much as possible. Thankfully, two days later, Monday, I got a call back from the manager who had interviewed me. I'd been offered the RN job at Nashville Medical Center.

After a week on the job, I was already exhausted, but loving every minute of it. The best part is, it kept my mind off Jake. As much as I didn't want to admit it, thoughts of him filled my mind way too often. There'd been something there between us, more than just an intense attraction, moments of something deeper which wasn't easy to forget.

When the next Friday rolled around, I was sprawled out on the couch in a t-shirt and sweatpants with a tub of popcorn and a good Netflix movie I'd been anxiously waiting to come available. Nix came down the steps dressed in his usual black boots, worn jeans, and his Club colors.

"You guys having a party tonight?"

"Yeah, you should come."

"I'd rather not."

"Guess who asked about you yesterday?" Nix picked up my feet, sat under them, then placed them on his lap.

"Dillon?"

"Jake." Nix let out an amused laugh. "He had the nerve to ask me how you're doing."

Affection kindled then sparked in my gut. I immediately doused that feeling and kept watching the screen. "That's nice. Did ya tell him to fuck off?"

"Sure did. Then he asked if Angela could stay at the Clubhouse."

"She's been staying with him all week?" My stomach did a loop-de-loop, and I swallowed down the lump that came up my throat.

"Must have been."

I stared at the screen, but I had no idea what preview was showing on it. My mind was thinking of Angela being at Jake's house all week and all the possibilities for their sexual relationship to spring back to life.

"Liz?"

"Hmm?" I turned my head to face him.

"Your phone is ringing." Nix pointed to it on the end table.

I glanced at the screen. "It's Jenna. I'll call her back."

"She probably wants you to come to the party with her."

"How's she know about it?"

"I told her about it."

"When did you tell her?" I eyed him with my sisterly suspicion, a smile creeping along my lips, swelling my cheeks.

"I invited her to it when she came last Saturday night."

"Hmm, guess you wanted to hang out with her again?"

Nix grinned. "She's all right."

I kicked my feet at his leg and smiled. "She's more than all right if you're inviting her to your party."

Nix patted my ankles before standing to get away from the conversation about feelings. "You should come hang out. You've been working hard all week. You deserve a night off."

"I'll think about it."

He headed to the door.

"Nix?"

"Yeah?"

"Did you let Angela stay at the club?"

"No. The moment Jake decided to stick his dick in her, she became his problem and no longer mine."

That was my brother, cold and hard on the outside because inside was a sensitive core he had to protect. He never showed emotion about anything except for when it came to me. I was my brother's weakness. It went back to when our mother had run off and our father told Nix he was going to have to become a man. Dad told him it was his job to help protect me. After Dad passed away, Nix took our father's words to heart and protected me like his life depended on it. He beat the shit out of any bully in school who laid a hand on me and threatened every boy who liked me.

When our Uncle Dallas took us in that protectiveness grew. No one was allowed to tell me what to do except Nix. By the time I was fourteen, he was no longer just my brother, but also my parent. Eventually, when Nix saw how much Dallas loved me, he softened and took a backseat as a parent and started enjoying his young adult life. After Dallas passed away, his parental instincts kicked right back in. He was the one who made sure I got an education after graduating high school and fixed up Dallas' Camaro for me to drive. Angela didn't deserve a man like my brother, but Jenna sure did. I picked up my cell and called her back.

"Sorry I missed your call. Nix and I were talking. What are you up to?"

"I was hoping you'd come to the club with me tonight. Ashley can't make it. She has to work and I don't want to go by myself. Pleeeease go with me."

"Yeah, I'll go. I can tell Nix is looking forward to you coming. I can be ready in forty minutes."

I rushed upstairs to get ready and was coming down the steps in a black, fitted, off-the-shoulder shirt, skinny jeans, and black knee-high boots when Jenna knocked on the door.

"Come in."

Her eyes widened at the sight of me. "Damn girl. You look smokin'. Trying to get a date tonight?"

I shrugged my shoulders. "I wanted to look good."

"Good? You look like you should come with a label called bottled sex. Every guy is going to want to have a drink of that," she pointed her finger at me and motioned up and back down.

A smile spread my lips. "You look good too! Love the straight hair. How long did that take?"

"Too long. You ready?"

"Yeah." I grabbed my keys and motioned her out the door.

When we arrived at the Clubhouse, I could tell it was already an active night. The music was loud and the parking lot was packed with bikes. We walked in and I couldn't help scanning the place for Jake. He was at one of the pool tables with his back to me. I turned the opposite direction and started looking for Nix and my Aunt May, but I hadn't moved fast enough. Trevor pointed my direction and Jake turned his head to look at me. His eyes locked on mine from several tables away, and yet, I still felt the heat of them on my body. I quickly avoided his gaze and followed Jenna through the crowd.

My Aunt May was at the same table as Nix. I kissed her cheek, taking the seat next to her. Nix pulled up a chair from another table and made room for Jenna to join us. When he put the chair next to him I gave Jenna a wink. She tried to contain her grin.

Aunt May patted my leg. "Nix says you got the job at NMC."

"Yeah. I love it."

"You must." She raised her bottle of beer and paused before drinking. "It's been keeping you busy. We haven't seen you all week."

"Work isn't the only thing that's been keeping me away."

"I heard," Aunt May frowned.

"What did you hear?"

"That Nix's ex decided to show her face again, but this time she's after Jake. She came with him tonight." Aunt May nodded her head toward Angela who was walking toward Jake with a beer bottle in hand. Jake took it, and she whispered something in his ear, then placed her hand on his ass and squeezed.

My gut wrenched at the sight of it. "I'll catch up with you later. I'm gonna get a drink." At the bar, I made small talk with Jeff and swallowed down a shot before I chased it with a beer. Dillon slid into the stool next to me and winked. His kind smile was refreshing even though he had ditched me the last time I saw him.

"I'm sorry I ran out on you last time. You seemed like you didn't want company, so I got out of there before it got uncomfortable."

I gave him a reassuring smile. "You were right, I didn't want company, but tonight I do."

"Good." His hand went to my knee. "You up for rescheduling dinner?"

"I am, yeah. Let's not do Italian though. Why don't you take me somewhere you like?"

"I know just the place."

"I'm off on Tuesday if that works for you."

"It's perfect." Dillon's smile widened. He ordered us both another beer and we spent a while chatting about how he ended up in Nashville, a little about his bike, my new job, and his sexy accent.

An hour later my legs were between his and his hand was farther up my thigh. I wiggled out of his warm hand to use the bathroom and glanced back at him, knowing he was watching my ass. He gave an unashamed grin and went back to chugging on his beer. I came out of the bathroom to find Dillon waiting for me in the hallway. He moved me against the wall and set his eyes on mine.

"I've wanted to kiss you for some time now." The palm of his hand took hold of my chin and lifted my lips to his. His lips were soft, skilled, and affectionate. He was a good kisser, but he didn't excite me. I was disappointed; I barely felt anything with his kiss. His lips were suddenly torn from mine. I opened my eyes to Jake slamming Dillon into the opposite wall.

"You fucking touch her like that again, and I will beat the shit out of you, brother or not."

"What the hell's gotten into you, Jake? Your girl's right out there." Dillon pointed toward the front room.

"Jake, you need to leave."

Jake's dark, brown eyes settled on me. He grabbed a hold of my hand and pulled me down the hall with him. His grip didn't loosen.

There was no way he was going to let me go even if I tried. He turned at the intersection and led me toward the offices and courtroom where the club members held their meetings. He opened the courtroom door and shut it behind us. My back was put up to the closest wall, his towering frame pinning me.

With one look in his hungry eyes, my frustration and desire instantly went to war. "What are you doing, Jake?"

His hand took hold of the wall, keeping me from slipping out. His other hand slid between my thighs and rubbed me forwards and back. My breath left me and my body tilted toward him.

"Jake," his name left my lips in a hot, needy breath, completely betraying me.

"This," he stroked me harder, "is mine. Don't let another man touch you, Peach. I'll put him in the hospital and I don't think you want that."

"What about—"

"What about no one?" His lips rubbed along my ear, followed by nips then sucking. "I've thought of you and only you, all week, Peach. I'd lay in bed stroking my cock, thinking about how you came apart for me that night."

Hearing those words ignited me. Like a scorching fire, my body was flaming with latent need for his touch. "I haven't stopped thinking of you either."

Searing kisses traveled down my neck to my collarbone. His hand took hold of my shirt and pulled it down from my arm and chest, exposing my breast. "Tell me what you want. I want to do it all to you."

His hand unbuttoned my jeans as his kisses trickled down my chest and nipped at the top of my breast. Slipping his hand into my jeans, his fingers cupped my soaking panties and rubbed them against my clit before brushing them aside and sliding his fingers into me. The moment he touched me, my body welcomed him, instantly moving against his hand, desperate for more of him. With quick, eager swipes of his fingers, he rubbed me until my knees grew weak and breathy moans escaped my lips. Freeing my breast from my bra, his tongue ravaged my nipple as his rough hand kneaded it in his palm.

"You don't know what you do to me," his voice graveled.

As his fingers dove and stroked, his tongue nipped and sucked. My head tilted back against the wall. I was useless, completely back under this man's control and I hated myself for how much I wanted him.

"Jake—"

"Say it, Peach. I want to hear the filthy words from your sweet mouth."

"Make me come, Jake. I want you to make me come."

"I love hearing those words from your lips."

He withdrew his fingers from me, grabbed my hips and pulled my legs up around his waist. His erection pushed right into me, and I tightened my hips against him as his lips covered mine, invading my mouth, and pulling moans from me with each breath I took.

My back hit the courtroom table and his hands were quickly pawing at my jeans, sliding them off my hips. His mouth came down on my opening, and with one slick lick of his tongue, he started from the top, slowly licked down, then back up, before sliding his tongue in, working me into a gyrating, mewling mess.

"This has to be what Heaven feels like."

"This isn't Heaven, Peach. There's no way a man like me would be allowed in."

His fingers slid in and stroked me greedily while his other unbuttoned his pants. He stood and lowered his jeans over his hips. His erection sprung forward hard, tight, and long. I reached for him, stroking him in my hand. He put both hands on the table and kissed and sucked along my neck as he thrust himself into my hand.

"Tell me who you belong to."

His words stopped me, freezing every part of my arousal like ice. I wanted to say I belonged to him, but did I? Or more importantly did he belong to me? Angela had to mean something to him, he'd had her at his house all week and brought her with him tonight. As much as my body was yearning to be claimed and devoured by Jake, I had to protect my heart. Irritated, I shoved him off me.

"I can't belong to you. You seem to already have someone." I stood and brought my jeans over my hips. "I think this was a mistake."

"Peach, don't leave." He quickly pulled his jeans over his hips and buttoned them.

"Even if you wanted to take me home, Jake," I turned back and set my eyes on his, "you can't. There's already a woman at your house. One you used to sleep with *behind* my brother's back and probably have been sleeping with all week."

"It only happened that one time, before I met you." He moved between me and the door.

"Are you serious right now?"

"Listen to me." He took hold of my arm and I yanked it from his grip. "I was drunk, Peach. I wasn't thinking. We were at a party. She came onto me. I was too damn drunk to turn it down."

"You... disgust me. *Stay* away from me." I tried to move past him, but he adjusted his footing, blocking me still.

"You're angry. You don't mean that."

"I mean it. My brother was right." I could feel the hot tears stinging my eyes. "You're an asshole. You don't give a damn who you hurt."

"Peach, don't walk out."

The door behind him opened. My gaze raked over the redhead behind him, then returned to him.

"Excuse me, Jake. Your girlfriend's here."

CHAPTER ELEVEN

LIZ

THE NEXT DAY, I held the phone to my ear, watching the light ahead and accelerating to get through the yellow before it turned red.

"What happened to you last night?" Jenna asked as I hurried home from work.

"I left early. I had a run in with Jake. We kinda got in an argument. I didn't want to hang out after that."

A loud pop sounded outside my vehicle and my steering wheel veered to the right. I dropped the phone, put both hands on the steering wheel, and slowed the vehicle to the side of the road.

"Damn it," I fumbled my hands around the floor of the car, looking for my phone. "Jenna, I'm going to have to call you back. I just got a flat."

I dialed Nix right away.

"What's wrong?"

"I got a flat. Can you come help me change it?"

"I can't. I'm in an important meeting. I'll have Pat send one of the members over. Where you at?"

I gave him the nearest street signs. Thirty-minutes later, I heard the rumbling of a Harley coming up behind my car. I got out and my body tensed. Jake got off his bike and approached my vehicle, looking all-too-sexy in a black tank tucked into jeans with ripped knees, dark sunglasses, his worn-out hat and black boots.

"Pat sent you?"

"I volunteered."

"No one else was available?"

"Not after I told them to sit the fuck down, no."

"You should go back. Send someone else. Anyone else. I'll wait."

"I'm stayin' right here." Jake's grin split his lips and that wicked tongue ran across his bottom lip. "Pop the trunk."

Watching Jake's massive arms flex as he pulled the spare tire and jack out of the trunk had me looking away in agony. He caught me, let out a breath, and winked at me.

"Stop it."

"Stop what?"

"Trying to be cute and sexy."

He set the tire down on the ground next to the flat and slid the jack under the car and started raising it. "I'm not doing anything, Peach. I can't help that you find me irresistible."

"Right!" I rolled my eyes and leaned against the car. "If I found you irresistible, we would've already had sex."

"We would've if Angela hadn't ruined it the night she arrived."

"And how is your girlfriend doing?" Just the sound of her name etched fire into my bones.

"You and I both know she's not my girlfriend." Jake put the lug wrench on. "I had her pack her shit last night and dropped her off at a hotel, like I should have done the day I left your house."

"Why didn't you?"

"I thought I owed it to her to help her out."

"Why?"

"It was my fault she ended up with the piece of shit who knocked her around. I ruined her and Nix's relationship because you're right, I'm an asshole. I thought the least I could do was make it up to her, but she wanted things like they used to be," Jake pulled the flat tire off and tossed it aside. "I don't."

Hearing him say that and knowing he made sure to be the one to come fix my flat was melting away some of the ice from the night before. He aligned the new tire and started putting on the lug nuts. Grease and dirt had gotten on his hands and arms. He glanced up and grinned when he caught me biting my lip while staring at him.

"Come to dinner with me tonight?"

"No. Taking Angela to a hotel doesn't fix everything, Jake." The words caught in my throat as tension swirled in my gut. "You betrayed my brother. If there's no trust, Jake, there's nothing. You know that."

Jake tightened the last of the lug nuts, lifted the flat, and carried the lug wrench back to my trunk. He grabbed a rag from his saddle bag and wiped his hands before putting it back. He walked toward the jack, but stopped in front of me first. Placing his hands on the car, he locked me in between his arms with my back against the passenger door. The hair on my arms raised. Every sensor in my body was ignited to his dominating presence.

"I'm not gonna stop until you beg me to fuck you, Peach. I told you, I'm not a nice guy, but I'll do whatever it takes to have you." His hand raised and thumbed my bottom lip as his eyes watched me fidget beneath him. "I think we both know you want me to have you."

My body couldn't lie to him. He knew just how to draw the need to the surface and make me weak with desire. I leaned in toward his lips as if to kiss him.

"You can start with apologizing to my brother."

Jake's jaw twitched. "I don't apologize to anyone, for anything."

"Then enjoy your dinner… alone."

A growl escaped his lips. His hand grazed my side, slid up and took hold of my ass and gripped it, pulling me even closer to him. "If I do this, you'll have dinner with me?"

"I'll consider it."

His scruff brushed across my cheek as he whispered, "Wear something sexy for me. I'll pick you up at eight."

He gave my ass a tight squeeze before he pulled away. He leaned down and lowered the jack and placed it in the trunk. After closing my trunk, he winked at me.

He got back on his bike and waited for me to get in my car and pull out before he did. On the drive home, I couldn't stop biting my lip from the stupid butterflies flapping in my stomach. There was something about Jake Castle. He'd gotten under my skin and permanently scarred me like a beautiful tattoo.

I had just gotten out of the shower and wrapped myself in a towel when Nix knocked on my door. "Come in."

"What did you do to Jake?" Nix leaned against the frame with his arms crossed.

"Why?"

"He came to my office and apologized to me today. Told me he's an asshole and that he never should've disrespected me by sleeping with my girl. He did call her a few choice words and said she'd come onto him, but admitted he fucked-up when he didn't stop it."

"And, what did you say?" Taking a seat on my bed, I looked up at Nix, a little too pleased with the news.

"I might be getting soft. I accepted his apology. The son of a bitch actually sounded genuine."

"Wow."

"So, what did you do?" Nix's brows pinched inward. "That's not like Jake to apologize for *anything*."

I shrugged. "He came to fix my flat today and said he'd taken Angela to a hotel, should've taken her a lot sooner, but was trying to help her out. He said he'd do whatever it took to get my trust and me, so I told him the first place to start was by apologizing to you."

Nix clicked his tongue, clearly surprised. "I'll be honest, Liz. It's obvious he cares for you in some way. In the four years I've known Jake, I've *never* seen him work for a woman's affection. They usually are throwing themselves at him, not the other way around."

My eyes dropped to the towel as I fussed with the loose thread, feeling unsure about my thoughts. Nix cleared his throat and I returned my gaze to his.

"Do you think I should go on the date with him tonight? That was part of the deal. If he apologized, I said I'd consider the date."

Nix's eyes narrowed as he studied me. "Be honest with me. Do you want to go?"

"A part of me does."

Running his hand through his dark locks, his gaze wandered around the room as he mulled over his thoughts. With a knot tight in my belly, he finally looked back at me.

"I'm not thrilled about it, but if it's what you want, then I'm not gonna stop you. Go on the date, but be careful. Don't let him off easy. He needs to earn his way into your heart and your pants."

"Thanks, big brother," I laughed, my smile spread wide. "Now get out, so I can get ready."

He started to close the door then opened it again. "Is it all right with you if I take Jenna out riding, maybe to dinner?"

My heart swelled in that moment. "Yes. Definitely. Take her."

At 8:01, the sound of Jake's bike rumbled up our driveway. A flutter of excitement swirled in my belly. I opened the door to him looking delicious in his black shirt with rolled up sleeves and jeans that contoured him perfectly. He looked me over and licked his lips before laughing.

"I should've known."

"What's wrong with this?" I waved my hand over my sweatshirt and baggy sweatpants.

"We can't get in with you looking like that."

"Can't get in where?" I was intrigued.

"You'll see." He looked me up and down and laughed again. "You were really gonna wear that?"

"No." I grinned. I lifted the sweatshirt over my head to reveal a fitted, black lace shirt with peak-a-boo sides. His eyes lit up and stared at my braless chest. His fixed stare remained on me as I wiggled out of my sweatpants to reveal maroon skinny jeans. I tossed the sweats on the couch and grabbed my knee-high boots by the door. I bent over and slid each leg into the boot, slowly zipping it up. Jake adjusted himself in his jeans, never taking his eyes off me for a second.

"Damn, Peach. You're killin' me."

As I stood up from the couch, he strode toward me and folded me in his arms. His hand took hold of the nape of my neck and his fingers got lost in my hair as he held me close and kissed me hard and passionately. His tongue slipped in and out only to come back again with even stronger need.

"Tell me you want me," his words filled my mouth. Taking hold of my hand, he placed it over the knot in his jeans. "I want you, Peach. I want to bury myself in you so hard, so deep, you come undone and beg me to take you again."

The sensations of the sharp nip on my lower lip and his calloused palm kneading my breast ignited my body. I could feel myself slipping into his web, being spun into a trap I wouldn't be able to escape.

"Jake." I put my hand to his chest to slow his pace. I caught my breath and nibbled my swollen lips. "We need to go... to dinner."

He let out a breath. "Right. Dinner." Taking my hand in his, he led me to the door.

We got out to his bike, he handed me his helmet before climbing on, and I slid on behind him. He wrapped my arm around his waist before starting the engine. At every light, he placed his hand on my leg and caressed it until the light turned green. These little moments of sweetness were taking my breath away.

Lowering my hand, I rubbed over his thigh, then slid my hand down to between his jeans and caressed him. He put one hand over mine and moved it the way he wanted it. I followed his lead and continued until a few moments later when we arrived at the restaurant. After parking, I climbed off and removed my helmet and set it on the back. Jake leered at me, then grabbed me and pulled me to the side of his bike. He patted his lap, indicating he wanted me to straddle him. I climbed on, and he pulled me against his erection, moving me over it as he claimed my mouth, ravaging me with his hands and tongue.

"Maybe we should go somewhere else. I can't keep my damn hands off you."

I sat back on my ass, putting space between us. "You're gonna have to."

"No, Peach. My hands are staying on you, but I will try to keep them in less risqué places."

"If you behave, maybe I'll reward you later."

"Let's get the hell in there and eat then. I want my reward."

As I climbed off his bike, his palm came down on my ass and squeezed. His hand slid inside my back pocket as we walked inside Soloman's Cajun Steak and Oyster, a place I'd only been to a couple times because the restaurant was pricey. As we looked over the menu, he put his arm around the back of my chair and kissed my temple.

"You're the sexiest woman in here. I was too distracted earlier to tell you how beautiful you look."

"Keep talkin' playboy. It's workin'."

He bit his lip and let it slide out between his teeth before grinning. "I'm pretty sure I smell peaches and cream lotion or something. You did that for me, didn't you?"

"Maybe," I teased, scooting my chair closer to his.

"It's a constant reminder of how much I want to put my tongue in that sweet pussy."

A sensation of pleasure started from the whisper of his lips on my ear and traveled down to the dampening part of me. His kiss came soft on my ear, then he leaned back to read the menu. I slanted my eyes at him and he winked over his menu at me.

I was afraid to be alone with Jake. My self-control and willpower were shriveling to a thin sheet as the night went on. He told me to order whatever I wanted off the menu, to ignore the prices, and again, he ordered dessert. I laughed when he raised the fork full of caramelized custard to my lips, taking turns feeding me a bite and taking one for himself. The gesture was intimate and sweet, and I couldn't help moving my chair right next to him and placing my hand on his leg, caressing the firm muscles.

"I've had a good time with you."

He wrapped his arm around the back of my chair. "I want you to come home with me."

"Jake, we both know what's going to happen if I do."

"You're afraid I'm going to lose interest in you once we have sex, aren't you?"

His directness caught me off guard. "I'm sorry, Jake. One dinner isn't enough for me to give you all my trust."

"What is?"

"Time and for you to prove I mean something to you, more than just a warm body in your bed."

"I don't want to go home without you." His eyes looked into mine and I saw something soften in them.

CHAPTER TWELVE

LIZ

"I mean it, Jake," I warned as Jake pulled me through the front door of his house with him. "You try, and I'm calling Nix to pick me up, and I'll let him slug you again."

"I promise, Peach. Give me tonight to prove myself."

Jake let Rocky out of his cage, and he immediately ran to me, waiting for me to pet him. After a scratch and a kiss, he followed Jake out back. I walked out behind them and got a good look at the fenced in backyard, porch, and grill. When we came back in, Jake told me to meet him in his room, he'd be there in a moment.

Jake came into the room with a bottle of beer in one hand, holding something behind his back with the other.

"What do you have?"

"I'm gonna need you to trust me, Peach," he replied, handing me the beer.

He waited as I drank some of the beer, then revealed what was behind his back. His hand came forward with black, silk eye covers and a covered bowl. I looked up at him, surprised.

"What are these for?"

"Stand up for me."

I stood, and he gently turned me away from him, the sound of the bowl being set down was followed by him sliding the cover over my eyes. His hands moved my hair aside and his kiss came soft on my shoulder.

"Promise you'll trust me?"

"I promise."

His hands continued down my arms and moved to my waist. His fingers slid under my shirt, gently pulling it over my head. His kisses continued along my neck as his hands inched into my jeans.

"Jake."

"You promised."

As his kisses continued, he undid my jeans and eased them over my hips. His body left me for a moment, then he raised me into his arms and laid me on the bed. Each boot was unzipped and slid off, then my jeans. I laid there on his bed, my heart beating in anticipation.

His touch returned and he ran his hand slowly along the inside of my thigh, following it with soft licks and kisses. The warmth of his lips reached my underwear and his kiss came sweetly before his hand moved it aside, making way for his gentle kiss.

His warm touch left me and I heard the bowl move. My stomach flexed at the first touch of the ice cube on my skin. He ran it along my belly button, following the trail of water with his tongue, covering the cold with his warmth. He put the ice cube to my lips, I sucked before it was removed and his lips replaced it. He gently pulled my bottom lip between his teeth and put his thumb to my lips.

"You have beautiful lips, Peach. Lips I want to feel around me."

I took in a breath when the ice cube touched between my legs. He swirled it around my clit, then followed it with his lips.

With ease, he took hold of my legs and turned me on his bed. His hands gripped my hips, raising my ass to him. His palm came down on me and I jerked forward from the surprise and pleasure of it. I bit my lip when another ice cube landed on my back, tracing along the center. The warmth of his mouth followed the ice cube and ended with him reaching between my legs and rubbing it against my clit. The ice cube faded and my hips rocked against his hand as he rubbed it over me. A gentle kiss was placed on my hip before he gripped it and rocked me harder as he slid his fingers in and out, rubbing against me, pulling desperate moans from my lips.

"That's it, Peach. Let go for me."

He steadied his hand and pulled me harder against his stroking fingers. I came apart, pounding into his hand, fisting the blankets in my palms.

"Jake…"

"Come for me, Peach."

I trembled as his hands continued to stroke and my orgasm rippled through my body. I collapsed onto his bed, moaning in pleasure.

He turned me on my back, his mouth coming down on my wet folds, licking and sucking at me feverishly. A second orgasm left me dizzy and panting. I was close to begging him for mercy when he pulled the covers from my eyes. His expression was pure satisfaction.

The taste of me touched my lips as his mouth claimed mine. With one hand, he took hold of my neck while the other took hold of my hip and rolled me onto my side with him. He looked me in the eyes with such fierce desire, I was nervous he wouldn't be able to hold back.

"I need you to touch me, Peach."

My hand went to his jeans as his mouth covered mine. I opened the zipper and reached in for him. He was swollen and rock hard and felt incredible in my hand. I stroked him several times before lowering myself, taking him in my mouth. His head tilted back and he fisted my hair in his hand and thrust his hips, eagerly pumping himself into my mouth. A growl escaped his chest as he reached his climax. I swallowed and licked the tip, cleaning him off. He shivered at my last lick and pulled me into his arms.

"These lips, Peach," his fingertip ran across my bottom lip, "they're my lips. This," he gently stroked between my legs, "is mine." His hand moved to my ass and squeezed it. "Also, mine. I licked it, Peach. It all belongs to me now."

I giggled at his declaration. "Does that work both ways?"

He pulled me down onto him and wound his fingers in my hair. "It does, yes."

"We'll see about that."

"You don't believe me that I only want you?"

"Time, Jake. I told you my trust isn't going to come easily."

Jake deadpanned and rolled me off of him and stood from the bed.

"Get dressed."

"What?"

"I'm taking you home."

"Why?" My heart sunk into my stomach.

"It's time to get you back."

His sudden change in demeanor made me uncomfortable. I quickly dressed in silence. The tension was growing between us, and I had gone from feeling like we'd made progress to feeling like the asshole had returned. I didn't say anything to him as I walked out of his house to his motorcycle. He followed, climbed on his bike, and waited for me to put on his helmet.

The tension continued for the entire ride home. By the time we arrived at my house, I'd gone through several emotions and settled on slightly confused and mostly angry. I stepped off his bike, took off his helmet, and shoved it at him.

"Don't bother getting off. I'll walk myself to the door."

He took the helmet from me and by the time I reached my front door, he already had his bike back on the road.

Entering my house, it was quiet at first then I heard Jenna giggling upstairs. I went to my room as quietly as I could, trying not to interrupt them. The stairs creaked and Nix opened the door of his bedroom a moment later. With flushed cheeks and messy hair, he smiled, but it quickly faded when he saw my expression.

"How'd it go?"

"Jake's an asshole," I snapped, before closing my door behind me.

Nix stormed in with his big brother face on. "Did he hurt you?"

"Not physically," I kicked off my shoes and ambled to the bed, "but emotionally he punched me in the damn gut."

"I think it's time you officially end things." Standing in the doorway, he crossed his arms, his expression displaying his disappointment. "He's playing games with you, and the longer you're involved with him, the more he's gonna be able to hurt you."

"You're right." I laid back on my bed, fighting the tears. "You're always right. Get back to hanging out with Jenna. I'm going to bed."

CHAPTER THIRTEEN

———

JAKE

I LEANED BACK in the chair and listened to Nix and Pat rattle on about club business, but their voices were drowning out in the background. I couldn't get Peach out of my head. I was still pissed she didn't trust me, but those thoughts were eclipsed by the memory of her lips wrapped around my cock, sucking me off the night before. I was getting a semi just thinking about it, and I wasn't a bit ashamed her brother was looking right at me. My lips raised into a grin. *That's right. Your sister sucks dick like a pro.*

"Jake, what do you think? Can you handle coverage as Sergeant of Arms on the fifteenth for the Riders Relay for Life?"

"I'll be there."

"That's it for business. Court is adjourned."

I leaned back in my chair and lifted my boots onto the table while Trevor dragged me into a conversation about whether or not he should upgrade his bike. A conversation across the table between

Dillon and Max kept pulling my attention away from Trevor. Dillon glanced at me and gave a shit-eating grin, then I heard Peach's name. At that point Trevor's rambling was background noise as I tuned into what Dillon had to say.

"I'm taking her out Tuesday night. That ass of hers. Fuck me, please."

My boots came down and I leaned over the table. "Tell me your dumbass isn't talking about my girl, right now?"

"Your girl?" A sound of amusement came out of his mouth. "If she was your girl, she wouldn't be going out with me Tuesday night. She asked Castle, so you must not be giving it to her right."

"I know I made myself pretty fucking clear." Anger surged from my gut, through my chest, and out my arm as it reached across the table and grabbed Dillon by the shirt, raising him out of his chair. "That's my girl, and if you lay a damn hand on her, I'll cut the fucking thing off."

"You better get your hand off me, brother."

"Jake!" Nix barked, his voice barely registering through my anger.

"I'm not backing off until you get it through that thick skull. She belongs to me. That's my girl. Keep your damn hands off." My fist exploded through the air and landed on his face faster than anyone could stop me.

Dillon fell back in his chair, holding his hand to his bloody nose. "You broke my nose, you son of a bitch."

"Jake! Get in my office, now!"

Nix slammed the door behind me. "That's your first strike. You know damn well there's no fighting unless it's fight night."

My adrenaline and smartass-odometer were sky high. "How's your cheek?"

"That's different, you shit. I hit you first, and you know it was way past due. What the hell was that out there?" Nix's thumb motioned over his shoulder.

"That was me giving Dillon a mental correction."

"A mental correction? What the fuck bullshit is that?"

"He seems to think that he's taking Liz out Tuesday night."

"If he's thinking it, then he probably is. I don't blame her either. You kicked her out of your house last night. My sister may not be quick to show it because she hides it well, but whatever the hell you did pissed her off. Actually, let me give you a mental correction. I listened to my sister cry last night... over your dumbass. So, yeah, if my sister wants to go out on a date with Dillon, she'll do what she damn well pleases. I wouldn't be so quick to call her *your girl* when I haven't seen you show her the respect and care she deserves! Be a goddamn man and tell her how you feel and claim her in front of everyone instead of hiding your relationship in your fucking bedroom!"

Nix turned toward the door. "And leave your damn colors on my desk. You're suspended from wearing them for a week."

With Nix out the door, it left me with nowhere to release my aggression. I needed to hit something, ride something, or fuck something, and I needed it now. After tossing my jacket into his chair, I walked out the front room and smirked at Dillon's swollen, fucked-up face. *That'll teach the prick.* I hopped on my Harley and headed to Peach's house. My knuckles pounded the door, but there was no answer. She was still at work, and I still needed a release. I got back on my Harley and headed downtown.

CHAPTER FOURTEEN

LIZ

ALL DAY AT work, I couldn't get Jake out of my head, no matter how hard I tried. The fact he hadn't contacted me or come by my house only added to my frustration. I couldn't understand why the switch had flipped the night before. I needed answers. I pushed open the front door and overheard the tail end of Nix's phone conversation.

"The arrangements have been made. It's all in the email. Notify me when it's done." Nix ended the call and looked at me uncomfortably.

"Was that the agency?" I asked, worried.

"It's business. Nothing for you to worry about." Nix pocketed his phone. "How was work?"

"It was good." I set my bag down by the couch and sat on the arm.

"You heard from Jake?"

"Nope. I don't know what the hell his problem is."

"I had to suspend his colors today."

"Why?"

"He punched Dillon after Dillon said he was going on a date with you."

"Oh my God, I forgot all about that. Jake was that pissed?"

"Broke his nose."

"Ugh, Nix, this is a mess. I need to go over to his house and figure out what's going on. One minute he wants me, then he's kicking me out, then he's punching Dillon over me. He's a freaking rollercoaster, and I'm starting to get motion sickness."

"Go over then. Figure it out. You two need to talk."

After a shower and something to eat, I got dressed in something semi-sexy and climbed into my Camaro. My stomach danced with butterflies over seeing Jake even though I was still confused about where we stood and what I meant to him. As I pulled up to his driveway, I sat for a moment, collecting my nerve. When I approached the door, I saw a light on inside, but no movement. I tapped on the door and there was no response even though his bike was parked in the driveway. I put my knuckles a little harder to the door, and finally, I heard Rocky shuffling in his crate as heavy footsteps approached the door. Jake opened it with heavy lids and a pungent smell of alcohol.

"Peach?" It was evident he was surprised to see me at his door.

"Can I come in? I thought we could talk."

"Now's not a good time."

Disappointment seized me. "Oh, um, yeah, that's fine." I heard footsteps behind him. Jake tried to limit my view by narrowing the open door.

"I'll come by tomorrow."

The sound of a woman's voice behind him brought a burst of anger rushing through me. I shoved the door open and saw a blond woman in lingerie stop abruptly. My eyes landed on Jake as the anger erupted like a volcano.

"Wow. You're a real piece of work, Jake."

"Damn it, wait." Jake reached out for my arm as I turned to leave.

I jerked my arm from his grasp as the tears welled in my eyes. "I don't know what we were, but whatever it was—we're done. You're such a fucking bastard."

He took hold of me and pulled me back to him.

"Don't touch me!"

"Peach, listen to me. She doesn't mean a damn thing to me. Nothing happened."

"Nothing happened? You were about to fuck her if I hadn't showed up!"

Jake's eyes narrowed on mine. "Suddenly I matter to you? I didn't seem to matter when you were making plans to take a backseat on Dillon's ride and suck *his* dick."

"What the hell did you just say?"

"Didn't think I'd find out? You want my trust, but it's fine for you to sleep with one of my brothers?"

"I made the date with Dillon on Friday when I thought you were sleeping with Angela. I completely forgot about it because that's how much he means to me. As soon as Nix reminded me, I had every intention of canceling it because I wanted to be with you. But I'm a fucking fool for thinking for one second that we could have something!"

"That's it, then. You're done?"

"I am." With tears in my eyes and my chest throbbing with pins and needles, I turned my back on him and got back in my car. I didn't look at him because I knew I'd lose it right there and needed to at least wait until I was home.

As soon as I pulled into my driveway, I lost it. I cried so hard, I was sobbing into my hands and the tears were soaking my shirt. I didn't even hear the front door open, but I did hear knuckles tapping on my window.

Nix stood outside of it motioning for me to come out. I tried to gather myself and opened the door. He opened it the rest of the way and gently pulled me out.

"Come here."

I folded myself into his arms and chest and cried it out. He patted my hair, wrapped an arm around me, and guided me into the house.

"You're done with him. I'll tell him and Dillon both to stay the fuck away."

"Can you call Jenna?"

"Yeah, I will." He opened the door for me and guided me to the stairs. I climbed them with what felt like cement bricks on my feet. When I reached my bedroom, I crawled right into my bed and sobbed into my pillow.

Thirty minutes later, Jenna walked into my room with two pints of Ben and Jerry's ice cream, a bottle of wine, and a duffle bag.

"Nix filled me in. Let's get drunk and bury our faces in ice cream." She dropped the duffle bag on the floor and crawled into bed with me before handing me a spoon and one of the pints.

I was halfway through my pint and my second glass of wine when I heard loud pounding on the front door. The pounding stopped when Nix opened the door, and Jake's voice bellowed through the house.

"I want to fucking see her!"

"Oh my God, Liz, he's here."

"Jake, you're drunk. She's not coming down!" Nix's commanding voice barked back.

"Peach!"

"Jake! Get your shit together, man. She doesn't want to see you. She found another woman at your house. What the hell were you thinking?"

I stood at the doorway of my bedroom listening.

"I wasn't thinking. I just want to talk to her. Damn it, Nix, get out of my way."

"Jake, she's *my* sister! And I'm telling you no. You're not coming in. She doesn't want to see you."

"I'll wait out here all damn night if I have to. Peach, come down here!"

My feet started to move toward the stairs. Part of me wanted to hear what he had to say, but then I heard Nix pick up my keys from the end table.

"I'm taking you home. You're too drunk to be sensible."

The front door closed and their voices drifted off into the distance. Jenna wrapped her arm in mine and wiped the stray tear from my cheek.

"What do you think he wanted?"

"I don't know. To apologize for being an asshole, for screwing up, either way it's too late for an apology."

CHAPTER FIFTEEN

LIZ

THE NEXT THREE weeks were difficult. I felt like the fight had put a rift in the club and my life. Because of Jake, I avoided going to the Clubhouse. While Jenna and Ashley continued to go and spend time with my family and friends, I worked at the hospital, hung out with a few co-workers, or stayed home by myself. When Jenna and Ashley came over, I'd cut them off when they talked about the Kings' club activities, making it awkward on all of us.

It didn't help that Jenna and Nix's relationship had grown. I was happy to see them together, but it was equally painful to watch. Every time Nix stole a kiss or affectionately touched her, it broke me to pieces. I missed Jake's touch; no, not missed, I craved it. I'd lie in bed thinking of what it had been like to have his fingers inside me or his tongue tracing the curves of my body, and I'd ache with need for him. Touching myself while imagining what he'd feel like inside of me was the only relief I could get.

I would wonder if he ever thought of me, and then I was reminded of the woman's face looking back at me in his living room. No doubt he'd moved on and buried his cock in countless women.

After lunch, I kept myself busy with charts, test results, and patient care and before I knew it, the day was finally through. I got home, showered, and thought about what I wanted to do. It was Friday and the Clubhouse was having its monthly fight night. I wanted to go, but I still had an underlying fear of seeing Jake in person. Instead, I ordered pizza and picked out a movie. An hour later, I'd gone through a quarter of the pizza and was dosing off and losing interest in the movie. A sudden call to my cell had me jumping awake. I reached over and grabbed it. Nix's voice filled my ear.

"I need ya to come over here and check Max out. He took a pretty hard hit."

"Have him go to the hospital. He probably has a concussion."

"You know how these guys are. He won't go. I need to you to check him out. Just give the okay or make him go to the hospital. He might listen to you."

"Fine."

It was loud and chaotic when I walked into the club. Everyone was surrounding the center of the front room, and I tried to look through the crowd to find Max. Nix found me and walked me over to where Max was sitting, his head in his hands, his elbows on his knees. I pulled a chair from the table and set it in front of him.

"Max, can you hear me?"

"Yeah, I can hear you." He slowly lifted his head.

"How many fingers am I holding up?"

"Three."

"Good. Have you thrown up at all?"

"Nah, spit up some blood. Busted my tongue on my teeth."

"How much have you had to drink?"

"Too much."

"You feeling sick or woozy now?"

"Yeah."

"Were you feeling sick or woozy before the fight?"

"Maybe a little."

"I'm gonna shine a light into your eyes, okay?"

Max sat still while I shined the light. His pupils were evenly sized and not enlarged.

"What did you have for breakfast?"

"Egg McMuffin."

"You don't seem to have a concussion, but I feel you should still get checked out. Especially since you're still feeling dizzy."

"Nah, if you think I'm fine, then I am."

"Don't drink anymore. If you have a concussion alcohol will make it worse. Got anyone who can pick you up?"

"Yeah, I'll make a call if I keep feeling like shit."

"All right," I smiled at him. "So, who'd you fight?"

"Jake."

My heart went into my throat. "Is he still here?"

"Yeah, he's fighting one of our new prospects right now. The kid probably won't make it out alive."

I stood and stepped onto the chair to see into the ring. Sure enough, Jake was in the ring, shirtless, with bloody knuckles and a dangerous, calculated look on his face. Another swing of his colossal arm and the new guy went down and didn't get back up. Watching him wipe the sweat from his brow and seeing the flex of his tatted muscles had my heart racing and my body responding viscerally.

I quickly stepped down before he saw me. With the crowd as thick as it was, I felt safe enough to hit the bar and get a shot to settle the warming sensation spreading in my body. Taking a stool in front of Jeff, I sat and chatted with him for a while. A couple other members' girlfriends joined me for a drink. It felt good to see my club family again and reconnect with some of the members. After another shot, I moved through the crowd and mingled before joining Nix at his table.

The crowd had settled, and Jake must have taken his money because no announcements were made. Club members went back to drinking, socializing, and playing pool. I did a quick scan and when my eyes landed on Jake at a table on the other side of the room, my chest tightened. I stood from my chair and patted Nix on the back.

"I gotta go. I'll see you at home." Turning toward the exit, I moved quickly across the room. Just as I was walking out, I felt a hand take hold of mine.

"Peach, wait."

The sound of his masculine voice sent a chill down my back. I didn't want to turn and look at those inviting, warm, brown eyes. "Jake, I'm sorry, I can't." I pulled my hand from his and walked out the door.

Back home, I stood under the hot shower, nearly in tears. The gentle touch of his hand and the sound of his voice had my mind completely wrecked. Thoughts of the way his touch felt lingered, warming me and torturing me, all at once. I wished he hadn't ruined what we had with his impulsive and stupid decisions because as much as I didn't want to admit it, I still wanted him.

After three weeks of analyzing everything that happened, I felt as though it wasn't all Jake's fault. I shouldn't have run to Dillon every time Jake made me jealous. I should never have asked for that date with Dillon in the first place; he was never who I truly wanted. I shouldn't have assumed Jake was sleeping with Angela while she was staying with him. I'd never really given Jake a fair chance. From the moment Nix told me not to trust Jake that's what I did. I never decided for myself if Jake was someone I could trust with my heart.

The last night we were together, Jake was asking me, in his own way, to open up to him, but I remained closed off, unwilling to let go and trust him. If I would've given him even a piece of me, he wouldn't have gone off the rail over Dillon, then turned to another woman. I didn't forgive him for what he did, nor did I think it was okay, but at least now I understood how he got there. Jake was far more complex than I'd realized. He wasn't the kind of guy to tell you how he felt. He spoke with action, and in his actions, he'd been telling me I meant something to him.

I stepped out of the shower and patted the towel over my hair to dry it, then wrapped it around me and brushed my teeth. At the sound of my bedroom floor creaking, I quickly spit into the sink and wiped my mouth. My chest tightened and I opened the door a crack to see who was in my room. My jaw nearly dropped at the sight of Jake sitting on my bed. I flung the door open and crossed my arms.

"What are you doing in my house, in my room, on my bed?"

Jake rested his elbows on his knees. "We need to talk." His glistening eyes kept lowering to where my towel ended at my upper thighs.

"I'm not sure I'm ready to listen." I walked to my closet and slipped inside.

"Damn it, Peach." His heavy boots thudded across the floor after me. "I know I messed up. I want to fix it." His eyes settled on me before he pulled me into his arms. "I need you. I've been a fucking wreck without you." His hand reached up and cupped my face as his thumb pressed down on my lip.

"Jake, please," I whispered, my arousal slipping through my voice.

"I've thought of these lips every single day for the last three weeks."

His lips crashed into mine with such fierce need, my body buzzed to life. He didn't let up and I couldn't pull away. We came up for air, my lids heavy, my body dizzy with lust. With one quick motion, he cupped my ass, raised my legs, wrapped them around his waist, and carried me the few steps back to my bed.

He laid me beneath him, pressing his growing erection into me as he growled into my mouth and claimed my lips. "I need to have you, Peach. Tell me you want me." His hand slipped beneath the towel and caressed between my legs. "God damn, you're soaking wet for me." His fingers slid in and my head arched back against the bed as my breath left me.

"Jake."

"Let me show you how much I missed you." His fingers stroked with unleashed desire, filling my head with fog, making my willpower grow weak. His hand cupped me as his fingers whipped over my clit, rubbing me into a moaning, wiggling, sexually dazed wreck.

"That's it, Peach. Come for me."

Once again, I'd lost myself to him. His control over me was undeniable. My body gave exactly what we both wanted. I came apart in his hand and moaned through my orgasm.

"Tell me you want me." His whiskey scented lips found mine and claimed them. His hand brushed along my side, caressing me gently. "Tell me you've forgiven me."

"Jake, I can't do this." Tears stung my eyes. "You can't hurt me and think you can make it better with sex."

His eyes looked down at me, pulling me into his magnetism. "I lost it when I thought you wanted Dillon. The thought of him having you the way I want to, I wanted to kill 'em, Peach." He put his head to mine. "I don't ever want another man to touch you like I do."

"What you did. I can't forgive easily. You have to earn my trust, Jake, and you can't fall apart when I don't give it at your pace."

"I'm an impulsive asshole. I can't be a nice guy for you, Peach, but I want to be the only man for you."

"This is how it always is with you. It's what you want when you want it. You're ready for us to get back together, so I need to accept you were going to sleep with another woman because you were jealous and pissed off. If I hadn't showed up when I did, you would have slept with her. You wouldn't have taken into consideration how that would've hurt me, how much it did hurt me to see her where I should've been." I pushed him off of me and stood, holding the towel tight around me. "I'm not ready to forgive and forget. I've completely lost trust in you. I miss you every damn day, Jake, but I'm not ready to let you back in yet."

His hands took hold of my waist and pulled me between his legs. His hand slid beneath my towel and caressed along the outside of my thigh as his eyes met mine.

"It's only a matter of time before I have you, Peach. I'm not gonna give up until I do."

CHAPTER SIXTEEN

———

JAKE

MY HAND REACHED for the door of Nix's office, but stopped when I heard the thick baritone of Pat and Nix's voices and instead stood outside and listened. Nix, being farthest from the door, was hardest to hear.

"Everything's in place. The deal is happening on Tuesday night. The bills are marked and when the arrest is made, they'll take down Tolito and every Wild Royal with him."

"I'm looking forward to these bastards being taken off the street. I feel good about this, Nix. You made the right choice to do it."

"I hope you're right about that," the apprehension in Nix's tone was clear, "I don't feel good about keeping this from the other brothers."

A chair scraped the floor, followed by Pat's voice.

"The less they know, the better off they are. The less chance of word getting out about the deal."

"The sooner this shit is over, the better I'll feel," Nix replied, his tone troubled.

The shuffling of feet had me rushing back down the hall, so I could turn around and make it look like I was just arriving. I nodded my head to Pat as he walked out of Nix's office and took his seat.

"We have shit to work out."

Nix sat back in his chair and rested his feet on his desk. "Let's hear it, then."

"I want her back, and I need to make shit clear. We need to let the past between us go. I don't want anything getting in the way anymore. I want her to know you approve. If you do, she'll trust me."

"Why should I approve?"

"You fucking know why."

"You love her."

"Every fucking bit of her."

"You gonna stop acting like a dick and treat her the way she deserves?"

"Let's save the father-son talk. You know how I feel. I haven't looked at or touched another woman in three damn weeks. She's the only one I want, and you know it."

"I'm not sure you deserve her."

"She's not your baby sister anymore, Nix. She's my girl. She's mine to take care of."

Nix's feet dropped to the floor and his chest came forward over the desk. "She'll never stop being my baby sister. Let's get that shit straight now. You fuck up even once, and I'll cut your goddamn balls off."

"I'm not gonna fuck it up."

"You better not. If you want my approval to be with her, you better damn well have your shit together."

"My shit's together. I want her and there's nothing getting in my way of having her."

"You better get ready to do some serious ass kissing, brother. You've done a piss poor job so far."

"Now that that's settled, we have other shit to discuss."

"What else?" Nix asked, leaning back in his chair.

"As the Sergeant of Arms, you should have me in on this deal you're working."

"How the hell did you find out about it?"

"Right time, right place. Now tell me what the hell is going on."

"After Bear's murder and May's assault, I started a working relationship with the Tennessee Bureau of Investigation. About three months ago, they approached me and offered a deal. They want to take down the Wild Royals and wanted our experience to aid them in the arrests. Their attempts at deals have failed and undercover agents haven't successfully been able to infiltrate the Club. You know how selective the Royals are about family members only, so we were TBI's desperate solution to a long-standing investigation of the Wild Royals' crimes.

"I was skeptical to do the deal at first, but Pat insisted. He feels we owe it to Bear and May. He's holding a grudge against the Royals for the death of his closest friend, and he's not the only one. It took my Aunt years to recover from her rape and the death of Bear. Liz doesn't even know about it. My Uncle Dallas wanted Liz shielded from knowing that kind of scum was a part of the MC community. He paid for his sister's therapy and helped her recover the best he could while keeping May's assault a secret, just as she'd asked him to. I have to admit I want to see them taken down too."

"Do you know who raped May?"

"The previous President, Tolito's father."

"This is deeper than I expected, Nix." I lifted my hat and rubbed the back of my head as I let out a breath to loosen the tight knot in my chest. "Your families have a long history of bad blood. Have you thought about if this deal with the Royals goes wrong that they'll want to retaliate, and who do you think they'd want to get their hands on first?"

Nix swallowed, I could see the wheels turning.

"Yeah, Nix, that's right. Liz is gorgeous. I know they've seen her growing up around the Kings Clubhouse. You'd have to be fucking blind not to notice her and everyone knows how protective you are of her. She's the perfect way to get to you."

"Jesus Christ."

"Is it too late to cancel this deal?"

"It is. Everything has been arranged. We can't back out now."

"I'll come by later to pick her up. She's staying with me until after this deal is done, and we both feel there isn't any chance of retaliation."

Nix nodded. "If she turns you down, I'll talk to her.

"I want in on this deal. I want to know every part of it, so I know how to handle what's coming. I'm not taking any chances of something happening to her."

CHAPTER SEVENTEEN

———

LIZ

IT WAS MY day off and Jenna and I had hung out most of the day until she ditched me the moment Nix walked in the door. She climbed him like a damn spider monkey before they disappeared upstairs. I went upstairs a few minutes later to grab the next load of dirty laundry, then headed back down to the washroom. My cell rang and I pulled it from my jean shorts pocket.

"Hey, Ash."

"I got your text. I can't believe he showed up at your house and was waiting on your bed."

"He looked so damn irresistible too. It took every bit of strength I had not to give in and fuck him senseless."

"I don't know why you two don't get it over with already."

I heard heavy footsteps behind me. I glanced over my shoulder to see Jake staring at my ass. Just the sight of him had my libido sparking to life.

"I gotta go. He's here." I hung up and set my phone on the dryer while giving Jake an expression of, *I know why you're here.*

He ran his tongue across his lips, his mouth twisting into a cocky grin. "I told you, someday you'd want to fuck me."

"Your arrogance is astonishing."

Jake's wicked grin widened as he eyed me like a delectable piece of candy he was about to unwrap.

"Finding you in here, without a way to escape, couldn't get any sweeter."

I raised my hand to his chest, pushing back the ripped, tatted beast of a man who was quickly filling the inches between us.

"Why deny it, Peach? The hungry look in your eyes tells me you want my cock buried deep inside you, begging me to make you come."

Fuck, he was right. But that didn't mean I had to admit it. At least not to him, anyway.

His arm raised, and his hand took hold of a loose strand of my hair, folding it around his fingers before giving it a tug, bringing my lips within reach of his. His breath left feather-like whispers across my lips.

"I think if I touch you here," his fingers traced up my inner thigh, sending a shiver across my body and up my back, reminding me what his touch did to me, "I'll find you wet and aching for me."

Damn, this man. He knows exactly what he does to me. Shoving his hand away, I padded toward the laundry room door, my only escape from the tiny room that had become a sexual sauna.

"Wait a minute, Peach," Jake's hand took hold of my wrist, stopping me in my tracks. "Don't leave." I turned to see genuine agony in his eyes. "I don't give a damn about any other woman. I want you to be mine and that's the fucking truth."

"I'm not yours to claim."

The expression in his eyes transitioned, darkening, revealing the caged beast within. "The fuck you aren't." His grasp on my wrist tightened, pulling me to his solid frame, enclosing me in arms of steel. "You're mine, damn it, and I'm gonna make sure everyone in this house knows it."

My loose tee was fisted in his grasp and ripped off me as quickly as my breath left me. His mouth slammed down on mine as he raised me by the hips and pinned me against the wall. His stiff erection pressed into my jean cutoffs, the only piece of clothing keeping me from what I knew would be paradise. His growl filled my ear as his tongue slicked wet kisses across my neck. "You don't know what you do to me, Peach, but you're about to find out."

My back left the wall and my ass landed on the washer. His shirt came off in seconds and my eyes were glued to his bare chest and the hands loosening his jeans, removing the black boxer briefs below. His cock sprung forward and my eyes followed the massive length of it to the shaven base, to his well-defined

Adonis belt, and back to the tip. This man was made of motorcycle fuel, ink, and rock-hard muscle, a cruel punishment to women, and I wanted to sin like never before.

His massive hands jolted my ass forward. I teetered on the edge of the washer and my own sanity. His quick hands undid my button and zipper as his tongue ventured in and out of my mouth, driving my arousal to an agonizing and desperate need.

My jean shorts disappeared onto the floor as my eyes met his fierce, predatory stare. With his hands on my knees, he spread my legs wide and looked down at me before lowering himself. His bold, brown eyes glanced up at me, hypnotizing me with his gaze.

"You're gonna come for me, Peach. I want to hear you scream my name."

Taking hold of my leg, Jake wrapped it over his shoulder and kept his promise. With his finger knuckle deep and his tongue whipping across my clit like a rapid-fire engine, I fisted his hair and begged for release.

"Oh... my... Go... please... don't... sto..." My body trembled as the orgasm shockwaved through my body. Jake lowered my leg and stood, his eyes locked on mine.

"We're not done, Peach. You still haven't screamed my name."

The taste of me met my lips as he took hold of my thighs and shoved himself deep within my wet folds. Lifting me with ease, he pinned me against the wall. With feverish need and unchained fury, he drove into me over and over, fucking me deep and taking me over the edge into complete and utter delirium. A deep growl escaped his chest as we neared our climax.

"Say it, Peach. Who do you fucking belong to?"

"I belong to you."

Jake fucked me hard, then groomed me with gentle kisses along my cheek, ear, and neck while still holding me pinned against the wall. He put his head against mine and let out a breath.

"You fucking shatter me, Peach."

I bit my lip and let it go between my teeth, still reeling from the ride.

"You belong to me. I want you with me every day. I want to bury myself in you every damn night." His hand cupped my face and his thumb pressed into my lip as his eyes softened. "I want you to stay with me, just for a while. I'm not asking you to move in with me."

This was Jake's way of putting himself out there again and I wasn't about to ruin it a second time.

"Yes, I'll stay with you."

A smile spread his lips before his mouth met mine, sweet and loving, a kiss of gratitude and affection. He pulled out of me and let my legs down.

"I'll help you pack. I want to have you at least three more times before I let you sleep tonight."

I laughed as I gathered my missing and torn clothes. "Who are you kidding? I'm not getting any sleep tonight."

Jake dropped my two bags by his bed and took me in his arms. "My house is your house. I want you to be as comfortable here as you are at home." I glanced at his bed and was going to say he needed to change the sheets, but to my amazement, Jake had already done that. He had an entirely new sheet set and comforter on the bed. A smile spread my lips and he kissed my temple.

"There's no way in hell I was having you back in my bed with the same sheets. I mean it, Peach." His hand raised my chin to him. "Nothing happened with her. I was drunk, angry, and jealous. I won't ever fuck up like that again. I promise you."

"Good," I took hold of his hands and pulled him toward the bed, "you can start making it up to me now."

"With pleasure." Jake lifted his shirt over his head, then slid his hands underneath mine and removed it. I glided my shorts off and climbed onto his bed. Sitting on my knees, I glanced over my shoulder at him. He removed his jeans and briefs before joining me on

147

the bed. He wrapped his arm around my waist and the other arm took hold of my neck as he licked and sucked at my ear. His fingers slid into my panties, caressing me.

"Anything you want, just say it, Peach. I'll do it to you."

I leaned my head back on his shoulder as he stroked my clit and sucked at my neck. "I want you to take me every way."

He pressed his erection into my ass cheeks. "Every way?"

"Yes."

His hand left my neck and fisted my hair, pulling my head back for him to claim my mouth. His kiss came filled with an unleashed and dangerous need.

"I want to do more than claim you, Peach." His tongue traveled along my neck and bit at the tender part of my shoulder. "I want to own every orgasm that comes from this sweet pussy."

His fingers dove and swirled, making me gasp with pleasure. With my hair fisted in his hand, he pushed me forward onto my hands and knees. His hands left me and clasped my panties, removing them from my hips, leaving them around my knees. I glanced back as he took hold of his cock and rubbed it over me, making the tip moist before burying himself in me. One hand took hold of my hip as he thrust deep and hard, pounding into me, while the other wrapped my hair around his fist and held tight as he worked to own the orgasm building up in me.

CHAPTER EIGHTEEN

LIZ

MY ALARM BUZZED on my cell phone and I reached over and cleared it. Jake's arm clasped onto me, dragging me back to him. As he pressed himself into my backside, his hot breath warmed my ear.

"Do you have time?"

"If you join me in the shower."

Jake moved to the edge of the bed and hoisted me off the bed into his arms. I giggled as he carried me to his bathroom. He let me down, and as I turned the knob to start the shower, his hand came down on my ass. I squealed and jerked forward, glancing back to see his devilish grin spread wide.

"That ass, Peach, will make a grown man a whipped pansy."

"You're screwed then, aren't you?"

"That I am," he agreed, squeezing my cheek.

I stepped under the water and Jake came in behind me, placing his hands on my waist, slowly moving me against the wall. His mouth met mine as his hand reached down and gently caressed me. This tenderness was the opposite of what we'd given each other the previous night. His back still bore the marks of my nails and surely I'd have bite marks to cover with makeup. With his fingers slowly sliding into my wet folds, my head went back as a slow breath escaped me. Soft kisses trailed along my cheek as his fingers wound through my hair and held tight to the nape of my neck.

Now filled with need, he removed his hand and placed it on my ass before lifting me off the floor. My legs wrapped around his waist as both of his hands took hold of me and pressed his weight into me, pinning me to the wall. He reached down and lifted his swollen erection and slid into me, covering my mouth with his. Whipping his tongue in and out, he ground his shaft against my clit, sending shocks of pleasure through me. His grip on my ass tightened as he pulled me forward and back, grinding me hard against him.

"Come for me, Peach. I want to hear you moan for me."

My held tilted back and my lips parted as the euphoric sensation swept over me. A moan escaped me and my back hit the wall as Jake gave one last hard thrust before his own orgasm claimed him. His head leaned against mine as his breath settled.

"I wanna lose myself in you every damn day."

My palm went to his cheek and caressed him. "I'll be home tonight. You can think of all the things you want to do to me between now and then."

Jake let my legs down and kissed me with his skilled lips. "You sure you can't skip work and stay in bed with me?"

"No," I giggled and reached for the soap. "I have patients who need me."

He took the soap from my hand and lathered it over my shoulder, arm, and chest. "I'll drive you to work. What time do I need to be there to pick you up?"

"Six. I'll bring a change of clothes, so if we want to go anywhere, we can."

"I already have a place in mind."

Making sure I had breakfast before leaving, Jake gave me a ride to work on his Harley. A couple of co-workers watched with peeping grins as he pulled me into his lap and kissed me before slapping my ass as I walked away. When he drove off, Sarah and Tracy waited for me to join them. Tracy pointed toward Jake riding down the road.

"Who was that hunk of meat?"

A girlish grin swelled my cheeks. "That's Jake."

"Boyfriend?" Sarah asked.

"Yes."

Tracy fanned her round, freckled face. "You are one lucky woman."

"I am. He rocks my world, one mind-blowing kiss at a time."

"Does he have any friends?" Sarah asked as we stepped in sync toward the entrance of the hospital.

"He does actually. Jake is a member of the Kings MC club. You heard of them?"

"I have," Sarah nodded. "Aren't they doing the Riders Relay for Life?"

"Yep, that's them. My brother is the President of the club. If you're serious about meeting any of them, I can take you to the next party with me."

"Not me, hun." Tracy raised her hand and wiggled her fingers. "He's balding, but I love him."

Sarah and I both laughed.

"I'd like to come. When is the next party?"

"Just about any Friday or Saturday."

"I'm in," she flashed her pearly whites at me and her blue eyes sparkled. "I'll check my schedule for my next weekend off."

"Great! Give me a call when you're free and I can meet you there."

After a long day of reading charts, test results, asking questions and caring for patients, my feet were killing me, and I was ready to see Jake. When I left my shift, he was right outside the hospital, leaning against his bike, his arm resting on the handlebars.

As I neared, he stood straight and reached for me, his hands wrapping around my waist and pulling me in for a kiss. I hadn't realized how much I missed those lips or how comforting they were until they shot electricity right through me.

"Ready to go to dinner?"

"Yes, please. I'm starving. I didn't get lunch today."

Jake handed me his helmet. "I'm taking you back to your favorite place."

"As long as you promise to feed me dessert."

"You like it when I put things in your mouth, don't you?" Jake's lips curved upward into a devilish grin.

"You're terrible." My stomach rippled with laughter. He got on his bike and glanced back, flashing me that same grin.

"You wouldn't have me any other way."

The bike rumbled to life. He was absolutely right, and I was falling for the impulsive, smart ass, sexy, hard shell of a man.

As we pulled up to Illano's, I felt Jake's muscles tense. He glanced at a couple of tatted bikers wearing Wild Royal colors coming out of the tattoo parlor across the street, then avoided looking their direction. I heard a whistle and someone shout. Looking over at them, I could see that they were calling to Jake and making their way across the street.

"Go inside, Peach."

"What's wrong?"

"Go inside."

I recognized that tone. It was the same one I heard before he and Nix got into a fight. My stomach bunched into a knot. I quickly set his helmet on the bike and headed toward the restaurant. I was yanked back by someone's fisted grip on my jacket. In my peripheral, I saw Jake take a hit to his face. He was off his bike in seconds and wrestling the guy who'd hit him to the ground.

Large hands took hold of my waist and spun me. My back slammed into a sign post, sending pain rippling through my spine and into my neck.

"You must be his ol' lady," A smoker's voice grated, putting the stench of stale cigarette much too close to my face. "I bet you're a nice piece of ass." His hand touched my inner thigh, and I shoved him away.

"Don't touch me!"

Jake's fist came crashing into the man's face. He buckled over and Jake spun and round kicked the guy, dropping him, face to cement. Putting the guy on the ground didn't stop Jake. He was on him in an instant, pummeling his fist into anything he could contact. Blood was splattering onto the sidewalk and people were starting to notice the fight.

"Jake, stop!"

In his adrenaline-fueled anger he didn't hear me. His fists kept slamming into the guy. I reached out and touched him. "Jake."

The contact shook him from his fury. He pulled back and worked on slowing his breathing. He looked at me, examined my face before pulling me into his arms and locking me tight against him.

"Did he hurt you?"

"I'm okay."

He put his bloodied hand to my face and raised my chin before accepting I was all right. He surveyed our surroundings, then looked back at me.

"We need to go. Cops will be here soon."

He helped me back on the bike and we took off toward home. Back inside Jake's house, he strode into the kitchen and grabbed a beer, downing most of it before setting it on the counter. He washed the blood from his knuckles while I ordered us food. As I set my phone down on the counter, he came to me and pulled me close. His touch sent a dull pain across my back.

"Owe." I reached for my back and slowly eased out of his grip.

His eyes darkened. "You're hurt."

I slid my jacket off and set it on the stool before turning my back to Jake. He carefully lifted my shirt.

"That fucker."

"How bad is it?"

"Take your shirt off."

I removed my shirt, and Jake took my hand, leading me to the bathroom. In the mirror I could see the gash across my back and the bruising of the surrounding tissue. Jake pulled out alcohol and gauze from his cabinet and poured the alcohol onto the gauze before carefully dabbing it on the wound. After a good cleaning, he placed fresh gauze and taped it. His anger hadn't settled. He was still steaming when he pulled my back to his chest and kissed along my neck and shoulder.

"If anyone tries to hurt you like that again, Peach, I'll kill them. I won't think twice about it."

The warmth of his body on my sore back was soothing, so were his protective words. "I trust you, Jake, with my heart and my life." I turned in his arms and his hand took hold of my face before leaning in to kiss me with a fiery need simmering just below his lips.

His hands cupped my ass and brought my legs around his waist before carrying me to his bedroom. He laid me down on his bed and kept his eyes on me as he removed every piece of clothing he was wearing.

I stared up at the face of the most handsome man I'd ever seen, one I knew would do anything to protect me. My eyes stayed on his as he undressed me. His kiss came with passionate, heated need as he ran his hand along my thigh until he reached my ass and held tight. His erection eased into me as he laid himself above me. His thrusts were slow and sensual, his lips trailed across my skin, biting and sucking, ending with gentle wisps of his lips.

The intensity of his touch and the sensation of every stroke of him filling me was consuming my heart. This man had claimed me from the moment he set eyes on me. I was never in control. He owned me from the start.

CHAPTER NINETEEN

LIZ

JAKE RAISED THE last piece of pizza in the air and motioned for me to take it. I leaned back against the pillow and shook my head. "You can have it."

Jake stuffed the last piece in his mouth and closed the empty pizza box before leaving the room with it. As soon as the bedroom door opened Rocky rushed into the room and came to the bedside. I waited until Jake was out of sight then lifted Rocky onto the bed. He nervously pawed at me and wiggled himself closer. Jake rounded the corner and stepped into the room. His footsteps halted and he crossed his arms as he leaned against the door frame.

"He knows he's not supposed to be in the bed."

I bit my lip and giggled as Rocky nuzzled his nose under my arm. "I let him up here."

"Peach," his tone was authoritative yet playful, "you can't spoil him."

"But he's so cute." I jutted my lip out.

Jake landed on the bed next to us and patted Rocky's back.

"We gotta remain a team, Rocky. Don't let her steal you from me."

I smiled as I leaned into his open arm and snuggled against his chest.

"Why were those Royals after you tonight?"

"The one recognized me. He was the buddy of the guy who gave me this." He motioned to the healed cut on his abdomen I'd stitched for him.

"That worries me. We don't need bad blood with them."

Jake was silent, clearly stewing in his thoughts. He pulled me tighter against him and kissed my temple. "Just for a little while, I want you to either be at the hospital, the clubhouse, or with me."

"You're worried about retaliation because of what you did to that guy, aren't you?"

His fingers bunched in my hair and caressed my head. "Don't ever worry about me. I can take care of myself. It's you I want kept safe."

Jake's concern wasn't unwarranted. I knew the Royals were dangerous. I had overheard enough of Dallas' conversations through the years to know.

"I'll stay close."

Jake motioned for Rocky to get off the bed. He quickly jumped down and followed Jake out of the room. After brushing my teeth, I snuggled under the blanket and waited for him to return. The sound of

Rocky's crate being closed was followed by Jake entering the bathroom, then moments later coming back to his room. Clicking off the lamp, he lifted the blanket and slid in behind me. His arm wrapped around me and pulled me against him. My breath became shallow as I relaxed against the warmth of him.

The next day after work, Jake was waiting for me outside the hospital, sitting on his bike with his ankles crossed at his feet, his arms folded across his chest. His black t-shirt was stretched tight and tucked into the front of his torn jeans. My eyes were glued to the mountains and valleys of his arms. When his eyes caught sight of me, whatever had him deep in thought evaporated. His expression softened, and he stretched out those massive, protective arms and pulled me into them.

"Have I told you how good you look in scrubs?" My lips caught his and an 'mmm' sound escaped him. "What is that? Some kind of berry flavor?"

"It is."

He tilted his head to my ear as he squeezed my ass, molding me to him. "That's not the only flavor of you I want on my lips."

A tingling sensation swam from my abdomen, down and back, awakening my arousal.

His head leaned back and a smirk crept along his face. "I may not ever let you go back home, Peach." His palm on my ass tightened, pressing me into the knot in his jeans. His hand raised and took hold of my cheek as his thumb pressed down on my lip. His eyes held my gaze, warming my body from head to toe before his mouth crashed down on mine.

I moaned into his mouth as his hand left my ass and slid beneath my shirt and pressed into my hip, slowly working into my pants. It took every bit of me to rein in my libido. I couldn't lose myself to him in a public parking lot right outside of my workplace. I took a breath and pulled back, giving him a pointed look. His grin widened.

"Did you bring a change of clothes?"

"I did."

"I'll wait while you get changed. I have somewhere private I want to take you tonight."

When I returned to him, his eyes started at my feet and followed my legs up to my waist, chest, then face. Reaching out for me, he fisted my hair at my neck and kissed my head. "You look gorgeous." He handed me his helmet and I bit back a smile.

I climbed on behind him and he glanced back to check on me before firing up the engine and taking off. Our first stop was one of the best burger and fry joints in town where he loaded food into one of his saddle bags before putting us back on the road.

The evening had turned to night and I curiously waited to see where he was taking us. The roads became less crowded and more curved as we traveled uphill. He reached a turn off and took us down a vacant, narrow road. His headlights and the moonlight were the only light illumination. We reached the end and he pulled off and dropped the kickstand. Ahead of us was an incredible view of downtown with bright lights scattered all across the darkened sky with the silver moon set high overlooking the city.

"It's beautiful."

Jake took my hand in his and turned me to face him. His mouth came down on mine with carnal need and passion that sent bolts of shocking arousal humming through my body. His hand palmed my ass and he pulled me against his growing erection as he growled into my mouth and ravaged my lips.

With one quick motion, he cupped my ass and raised my legs, wrapping them around his waist and carried me the few steps back to his bike. He sat on it with me straddling him and his hands roamed my waist as he pulled me over him, unleashing that same desire that was making my head fill with fog. Firm hands caressed my back, waist, and thighs as the thirst for more of him consumed me.

My shirt was lifted off and his lips came crashing back down on mine as he worked the button

162

and zipper of my jeans. My breath was already heavy as I moved myself forward and back over his erection. A growl filled my mouth, and he gripped my hips and pressed me down harder.

"I want it, Peach. I want to fucking bury myself in it."

He lifted me off his bike and turned my back toward him before sliding my jeans off my hips. His hand wound around my hair and bent me forward. My hands gripped his bike as his tightened on my hair, tilting my head back. His mouth came down, biting at my hip as his hand slid off my underwear and reached inside me. My breath left me as he stroked and rubbed, working me into a frenzy with trembling knees and loud desperate moans. More nips and bites trailed along my shoulder as his erection pressed into my ass cheeks and his hand drew my orgasm from me.

"I want to hear it, Peach. Come for me."

A whimpering moan came from my quivering lips as the pleasure of my orgasm released. Behind me, his zipper came undone and moments later the tip of him was rubbing against me, taunting me.

"Tell me you want it." His hand tightened in my hair and pulled my head back as he slid in then pulled out, drawing out my agony.

"Fuck me, Jake. I want it now."

With one swift motion, he filled me deep and gripped my hip as he repeatedly thrust into me, smacking my ass cheeks against his pelvic bone. A groan escaped him as he swelled inside me.

"This tight pussy, Peach. You fucking destroy me." With one deep thrust his orgasm exploded from him and his tight grip on my hair released as he let out a moan. Gentle nips were followed by his lips kissing along my shoulder. Raising me off the bike, he wrapped his arms around me, taking my breasts in his hands, kneading them as he licked and kissed my neck.

"I've never wanted a woman so much in my life. You own it, Peach. It's yours."

The tenderness in those words filled me with an intensity I'd never felt before. I turned my head to him and met his lips. His hand held my hair and neck as his mouth passionately moved against mine. My tidal wave of emotions traveled to my heart and lingered there, pulsing intensely.

"You own all of me, Jake. I'm completely in love with you."

His head fell against mine. "I don't take those words lightly." He took a breath and his jaw tensed. His fingers strummed through my hair and brushed it over my shoulder, out of his way. Sweet, soft kisses brushed across my shoulder.

"The way it feels to have someone who is mine. I never thought I needed it." His hand stroked along my waist and caressed my hip as his kisses traveled from my neck to my cheek. "But now that I have you, I know what I've been missing."

164

I laid down a small blanket Jake had packed in his saddle bag while he brought over our food. As he settled onto the blanket next to me, I moved as close to him as I could get. He looked at me and winked before placing a french-fry to my mouth. I nibbled it out of his hand, making him laugh.

"As I'm sitting here thinking, I realized I've fallen in love with a man, and I don't even know what you do for a living."

Jake's smirk raised the corner of his mouth. "I'm an escort."

My jaw dropped and I gaped at him. "Are you serious?"

"Would you love me less if I am?"

Nausea churned in my stomach as my emotions spun in turmoil.

"Relax, Peach," Jake laughed and shook his head, "I'm not an escort."

A breath of relief escaped me. "You're an ass."

"It's part of my charm." Jake caressed my thigh as he fed me another french-fry.

I laughed and leaned into him. "What do you do?"

"I own the jujitsu shop on Seventh."

It made perfect sense now why he was solid muscle and could fight like a warrior.

"How long you been doing it?"

"Eight years. Started when I was twenty-one. I moved here from Georgia to get a fresh start and the place was for rent. I paid the first few months in advance and got the shop up and running. I have a manager running things for me now. I do some one-on-one training on Tuesdays and Thursdays and stop in when I feel like checking on things or getting in a workout."

"I've driven by that place. It's always packed."

"I got a gym in there too. A lot of people use it to work out."

"When you say fresh start, are you talking about what happened with your family?"

"Not just them." Jake's eyes darkened. "A different family. I used to ride with an outlaw gang until I saw a buddy of mine get murdered. After that, I took off. Didn't know where the hell I was going, but I needed out. I wanted to leave behind everything and figure out what I was doing with my life. When I came here, I ran into Nix and Trevor at a bike show and they offered for me to prospect for them. I took my new family for granted though. Until you."

Wrapping his arms around me, Jake pulled me into his lap. His hand held my face as his eyes settled on mine. His kiss came with a fiery need I hadn't felt before as if he'd let his emotions lose from a place they'd been caged in until now. Laying back on the blanket, he pulled me down with him. His hands held my ass tight against him, moving me over him as he moaned into my mouth.

"I want you to ride me."

"With pleasure." A wicked smile crossed my lips as I lifted my shirt over my head.

CHAPTER TWENTY

——

JAKE

AFTER DROPPING PEACH off at the hospital the following morning, I went to my shop to sign paychecks, get updates on operations, and for the one-on-one training. Afterward, I headed to the Clubhouse to see Nix. He was in his office finishing a call when I walked in.

I landed in the chair opposite him. "I got your text last night. The deal is happening tonight?"

"Yeah, in the parking lot of an abandoned warehouse on Fifth. How's Liz?"

"She's good." A smirk spread my lips as the memories of the night before flashed through my mind. "She's with me at all times when she's not at the hospital. You need to know, I have no intention of bringing her back home to you."

Nix's eyes widened before his lips spread in humor. "Sounds like my sister has you wrapped around her little finger."

"Damn right, she does. I thought about having you order her a property shirt."

"You know she won't wear that shit," Nix laughed.

"I know it. I made a joke about her being my ol' lady. She slugged me and told me that title is for old, married, biker wives."

"Jenna feels the same."

"You two together?"

"Yeah, but she knows something's up."

"What are the plans tonight?"

"Activity as usual. I don't want any chance of suspicion."

"Who's doing the deal?"

"The Devil's Slayers are purchasing the drugs on behalf of an anonymous buyer."

"And we're the anonymous buyer?"

"We are. The bills are marked. The Devils have been given a location to drop the money in exchange for the drugs. Their payment will be given to them and they'll be none the wiser. TBI has checkpoints set up at every possible exit. When the Royals are arrested, the marked bills will be confiscated."

"How did you know the Devil's would take the offer from the anonymous buyer?"

"Pat knew that the President, Otto, is about to lose his business. He's desperate for the money."

"Won't the Royals think the Devils rolled on them?"

169

"That's why the checkpoints. They're not going in busting a drug deal as if they knew about it. It's a higher risk for the TBI, but it's the only way I'd agree to set this deal up for them."

"This damn deal needs to be done." I leaned back in the chair, stretching the knot tightening my chest. I lifted my hat and rubbed the back of my head. "Damn it, Nix. If this fails, if the Royals find out you were the anonymous buyer, there'll be hell to pay."

"I know, Jake. Just do what you promised and keep my sister safe. I'll handle the rest."

"This deal isn't the only potential problem we have with the Royals."

Nix's jaw tightened. "What the fuck did you do?"

"I took Peach to Illano's. The buddy of the bastard who beat on Angela recognized me. Him and his brother jumped me."

Nix's green eyes darkened. "Did they touch Liz?"

"The one fucker got his hands on her for a moment before I broke his face."

"Fucking Angela. She's been nothing but trouble since she walked in here with Mick. I understand why you put her ol' man in the hospital, but now this." Nix ran his hand through his hair. "I hope every one of those shits gets arrested tonight. We don't need to be looking over our shoulders waiting for them to retaliate."

"I'll keep her home with me tonight." I stood to leave. "I want to know everything you know, right after you hear it."

Nix nodded and I could see the stress of this situation in his tired eyes. "I'll keep you informed."

I left the clubhouse and headed to the hospital to pick up Peach.

I waited the few minutes it usually took her to walk out; the nerves in my gut started jack-hammering when she didn't come. I checked my phone. I'd missed a call from her. Swiping the screen, I called her back.

"Hey, Jake."

"Peach, where are you?"

"I tried to call you. Jenna picked me up from the hospital early. We went into town."

"You told me you'd stay close. What are you doing in town?"

A giggle escaped her, then I heard the sound of a tattoo needle buzzing. "You should come to Ink and Ice and find out."

I hung up and took off on my Harley, making it there in twenty minutes. I walked in and removed my shades. Two tatted guys were sitting at the front desk.

"Where's my girl? Gorgeous brunette, getting a tattoo."

The bald one with gauges in his ears pointed to the back. "Third one on the left."

I turned the corner and found Peach laying out on the bed with her hip bare and the artist finishing up the outline. She was taking it like a champ. No doubt the endorphins had kicked in at this point. She was only flinching when he hit the most tender areas.

She and Jenna both looked up at me with proud grins.

"A tattoo, huh?"

The artist looked over his shoulder and nodded. "Hey, man."

I nodded before moving into the room for a closer look.

Peach bit her lip, her cheeks turning pink. "I've wanted another one for a while and now seemed like the right time."

As I moved in closer, I noted the details of the swirls, dots, and flowers. Hidden in the details were the letters JC. A grin split my lips. This permanent sentiment I'd always see on her body filled me with more pride and ardor than I'd ever experienced.

"It's gonna look sexy as fuck on you, Peach. I love it."

Her smile spread wide beneath her sparkling green eyes.

I winked at her before turning toward the exit of the room. "I'll be back. Take care of her, Jenna."

Returning to the front desk, I leaned against the counter. "Either of you available to do a tattoo?"

The bald, tatted guy with gauges lifted his head from his phone. "Sure man. What do ya need?"

"In cursive, I want the name, Peach."

"Easy enough." He grabbed a sheet of paper and a pen and set them on the counter. "Put your initials on each line, then sign on the bottom." The guy took my signed sheet, put it away in a file, and stood from his seat. "I'm Louis. My room is the first door on the left."

Louis came in behind me as I sat on the bed. "Where do you want it?"

I raised my shirt and pointed to the right side of my abs just below my current tattoos.

His gaze raked over my current ink. "You want it in black?"

"Yeah."

Twenty minutes later the tattoo was done. I paid at the counter and went back to the room Peach was in. She was squirming a bit more now that he was filling in the shading.

"How you doing?" I moved around Jenna and pulled a chair over to Peach's side.

"Better now that you're here."

I brushed my fingers over her bare stomach and watched the arousal fill her eyes.

"Where'd you go?"

"Had to take care of something important. I'll be here for the rest of it. You still got a while before he's done."

An hour and a half later, Peach stepped off the bed and stretched her stiff muscles before standing in front of the mirror and checking out her tattoo. I watched her turn her ass and already was imagining her naked with the new tattoo.

"It looks amazing!" Jenna praised.

Peach's cheeks swelled as she stared at it in the mirror. "You like it?" Her eyes caught mine.

"I more than like it. Didn't think you could get anymore gorgeous than you were, but that tattoo proves me wrong."

She moved across the room and slid into my lap. My semi pressed into her ass and she gave me a knowing look.

Her tattoo artist went through the usual spiel about what she needed to do to take care of it. I kneaded my thumb around the tattoo as she listened intently. He walked out of the room and she leaned into my chest.

"I'm gonna call Nix." Jenna stood and pulled her phone from her purse. "See you in the lobby."

She walked out, and I brought Peach closer and devoured her sweet lips with mine. Reaching down, I cupped between her legs and rubbed her. She moaned into my mouth and I stopped before I took it too far.

"As soon as we're home, I wanna show you how much having my initials on your body means to me."

"I'm looking forward to it." Her bright green eyes lit up. She rubbed her palm over my junk, expelling a growl from my chest.

"Damn it, Peach. I need to get you home, now."

"Can we pick up something on the way home first? I'm starving."

"Yeah. Let's go."

My palm came down on her ass as she stood. No doubt everyone heard her squeal. She glanced over her shoulder at me with a lascivious grin as she rubbed her hand over her cheek. My hand took the place of hers as we walked out to the lobby. I pulled my wallet out and tossed my card onto the counter.

"Jake, I didn't call you here to pay for my tattoo."

"Hush, Peach. I got it."

She eased her body under my arm and caressed my back, sending pleasurable chills across my skin. "Will you rub me like that later?"

She looked up at me with affection in her eyes and smiled. "Yes."

I signed the receipt and put my card away. Jenna joined us at the counter just as we finished.

"Nix said he wants to see your tattoo. A bunch of members are going to the clubhouse tomorrow night. He wants you both to come."

"We'll be there," I assured her.

Jenna left to go to Nix's house and I took Peach home on my bike. On the way, we picked up carry out from a local Asian place she liked. She set out the food while I took Rocky out. When I came back in, my eyes caught sight of her shirt rolled up and her pants folded off her hips. Seeing the dark ink etched across her skin, traveling in hypnotic swirls around her curves, was intoxicating. Her dark, loose waves cascaded down her back, and I found myself fisting the soft length of it in my hand as I tugged. Her head fell back as my lips claimed hers.

"The food can wait, Peach. I can't."

My hand took hold of her thigh and turned her to face me. Both hands gripped her ass and pulled her off the stool into my arms. Her toned thighs gripped my waist as she slid her tongue between my lips. My fingers hooked into her underwear, pulling them down with her jeans. I sat her bare ass on the counter and worked each leg out of her pants. Her shirt disappeared mid-air as I removed mine. Eagerly, her hands took hold of my belt as my stiff cock pressed against my jeans. Her hand dropped my fly, disappearing inside my briefs. Her warm hand closed around me and stroked me before releasing my throbbing erection.

With her fist wrapped around the length of me, I thrust into her hand while ravaging her berry flavored lips. Pumping me hard in her hand was taking me too close to the brink. I took her hand in mine.

"Not yet, Peach. I need the taste of you on my lips."

I lowered her onto the counter, watching her green eyes blaze with desire. Taking hold of her legs, I wrapped them over my shoulders as I placed my mouth on the sweetest pussy I'd ever tasted.

A small, dark patch left plenty of room for me to see what I liked—pink, swollen lips aching for me to claim them. My tongue dipped into her tender folds and a needy whimper escaped her.

"You want more?"

"Please, Jake... make me come."

"That's right, Peach. I make this pussy come, only me."

My tongue dove into her and fell into a rhythm of flicks and swirls as her hips bucked and her fist clenched my hair. Sliding my middle finger in knuckle deep, I found her soft center and stroked, giving it the needed momentum to tip her over the edge. Breathy, desperate moans sounded in my ears, then with one brief exhale the warmth of her filled my mouth.

I let her legs down and wiped the taste of her from my lips. Taking my throbbing cock in my hand, I rubbed it along her moist clit before pushing into her tight folds. Her walls clenched around me and a groan rolled out of my chest. Nothing had ever felt as good as being inside of her. I could never seem to get enough. Gripping the outside of her thigh, I pulled out slowly then thrust deep, filling her to the base.

Her eager whimpers grew louder as the pace of my strokes increased. I buried my cock deep into her cavity and with each thrust, her muscles clenched around me, tightening my groin as my own orgasm shot through me.

"You feel so damn good."

Her hips lowered as she let out a breath and the warmth of her orgasm poured over me. I continued to move against her, giving her every last bit of pleasure I could. A satisfied smile swelled her cheeks, and she raised herself to my lips. Her hands took hold of my face as she placed her head against mine.

"I fucking love you, Jake Castle."

A grin spread my lips. "You better fucking love me. Cause I fucking love you, Peach."

I claimed her lips and held her tight against me, not wanting to lose this moment or the warm, fuzzy shit swirling around my heart.

She lifted her head from mine, her hands brushing along my chest as she leaned back to admire me. I couldn't help grinning from ear to ear when her eyes shot wide and she gawked at the new addition to my ink.

"Jake! When did you do that?"

"When I slipped out for about thirty-minutes during yours, that's what I was doing."

"Oh my God."

Tears pooled in her eyes when she looked up at me with those soft, seductive, green eyes. The same eyes that had captured me from the very first moment I saw them.

"You glad I got it?"

"I love it." Her arms flung around me and she buried her face into my neck. "I seriously love you."

I lifted my hand and raised her chin to me. "The shit you do to me, Peach." I swiped the tear rolling down her cheek. "I'd do anything for you."

Later in the night, after we finished our reheated food, and I put lotion on her tattoo, I laid in bed next to her, holding her against me, listening to her breathe as she slept. Tension clamped my chest tight as I waited to hear from Nix. This deal needed to go as planned and the Royals put behind bars. The woman lying next to me had finally given me something to live for, and I'd be damned if I let anyone ever hurt her. The light on my phone finally lit up, indicating a text had come in. I quietly moved off the bed and took the phone into the spare bedroom, closing the door behind me.

"What do you know?"

"The deal went down as planned and the Devil's received their money. There's one problem."

"What?" I clenched my fist as my jaw tightened.

"Tolito's crew has been arrested, but Tolito and two of his members disappeared. TBI says they must have taken a route the TBI didn't know about or they're hiding somewhere."

"Son of a bitch."

"Keep this shit under wraps, Jake. As far as Tolito knows, his crew was arrested at a standard checkpoint for the possession of stolen guns and illegal drugs."

"Business as usual, then?"

"Yeah. Bring Liz to the clubhouse tomorrow. I wanna see her. And who's fucking idea was it for this tattoo?"

"Hers." A chuckle escaped me as I grinned. "She's got my initials on her now."

"Wipe the fucking smirk off your face. See you tomorrow."

CHAPTER TWENTY ONE

———

LIZ

SITTING ON JAKE'S bed, I held up two different shirts. "Which one should I wear?"

Standing in his closet in just his briefs, Jake glanced over his shoulder. "The shorter one, it shows off the tattoo."

I bit my lip and smiled. "You don't mind your brothers seeing some skin?"

Grabbing a pair of ripped jeans and a tank, he turned to face me and chuckled. "Hell no, I don't mind. I want them to see what's mine."

I stepped into the closet just as he brought his jeans over his hips. I moved into his space and slid my hand into his briefs. My lips grazed his. "And this is mine." My hand glided over the length of him, pumping him in my fist. His hands took hold of my arms, gripping hard as he lost himself to the feel of my touch. "If any girl tries to take what's mine, I'll claw her fucking eyes out."

A hiss escaped his mouth as he bit down on his bottom lip. I withdrew my hand to get his briefs and jeans off his hips. His hand fisted my hair and his other hand took hold of my shoulder and lowered me on my knees. With his erection in my hand, I brought him to my mouth and licked at the tip. His hand tightening on my hair, he pressed himself against my lips. My tongue teased the tip.

"Tell me you want it."

He pulled my hair back and lifted my chin. His intense brown eyes stared down at mine. "Put those pretty little lips on my dick, Peach, and show me how much you love it."

I opened my mouth to him and held him at the base as I brought him in and out, sucking hard. His grip tightened and his head rolled back as he thrust himself into my mouth and slid his cock to the back of my throat.

"Fuck, Peach."

Several more thrusts into my mouth had him losing control. I held tight, moaning and sucking, devouring him one inch at a time. The taste of him poured into my mouth as he let out a satisfied groan. His eyes met mine as I swallowed.

His hand raised and feathered across my cheek. "That mouth, Peach."

I stood and he pulled me into his arms. His scruff grazed my cheek as his lips nibbled my ear. "I wanna be inside either this ass or pussy."

One hand caressed between my legs as his other squeezed my backside. His teeth scraped my neck before biting and sucking a trail to my shoulder. My body was weakening, scorching arousal already burning between my thighs. His lips brushed across my skin.

"Where do you want it?"

"You know where."

A low, sensual moan filled my ear. "That's where I thought." His grip on my ass tightened. "Get on the bed and strip. I wanna see that ass before I bury myself in it."

Over an hour later, Jake opened the door of the clubhouse and guided me in. His arm was clamped around me, holding me close. When several gazes shifted our direction, Jake placed his hand on my cheek and turned my head to face him. His lips met mine, giving a kiss that told everyone I was his.

When our lips parted, I held tight to him until the light-headed feeling passed. He winked at me and pulled me along with him to Nix's table. Nix stood and reached out his arms, stealing me from Jake.

"You go to Jake's, and now I never see you."

My cheeks flushed. "I'm sorry. We've been busy."

Nix's eyes swept over Jake and narrowed before returning to me. "Let me see the tattoo."

I lowered my jeans, revealing the bottom half of the tattoo. Nix's eyes raked over it. He studied it closely, and I was sure he saw the initials. His eyes fell on Jake again and Jake's grin spread wide. Nix rolled his eyes and returned his gaze to me. "It looks good."

Jake's arm wrapped around me and pulled me to him, giving me a kiss on my temple. Everyone watched the affection with astonished expressions.

"I'm getting us both a beer."

As Jake disappeared into the crowd, the eyes of everyone at the table settled on me. Trevor's mouth twisted into an impish grin.

"What'd you do to him, Liz? I've never seen him like that with a woman."

Nix turned his head over his shoulder and shot daggers in Trevor's direction. Trevor's mischievous grin spread as he brought his beer to his lips. Max patted Trevor on the back.

"Let's get Jake and play some pool before Nix knocks your ass out." The guys left the table, and a moment later, Jake came by and dropped off my beer before joining them.

"He really is being attentive to you." Jenna's smile widened as I took the seat next to her.

My cheeks warmed as my smile stretched my lips. "We both said the L-word."

Jenna wiggled in her seat. "I'm so happy for you!"

"I feel the same. You and Nix?" I motioned my thumb over my shoulder in his direction.

Jenna's hand grabbed my arm and squeezed as her cheeks turned pink. "I'm crazy about him."

"I can tell he's really into you, too."

"Really?"

"Yes. I promise you. I know Nix isn't the best at showing emotions, but I know my brother, and he's smitten."

Jenna's big brown eyes lit up. "You don't know how happy that makes me feel."

I reached out and rubbed her shoulder. "I do know."

Jenna's eyes left mine and froze on someone behind me. I glanced over my shoulder to see Dillon walking in. Looking through the crowd, I caught Trevor's nod to Jake, and then Jake's gaze went to Dillon.

"Nix said they got in a fight. Apparently, they're still pissed at each other." Jenna turned her attention to Jake. "He's watching Dillon like a hawk."

"I hope he doesn't come talk to me. Jake will flip."

"No, he's looking at you now, but heading toward the bar. There's a couple guys waving him over."

"Good."

"Jake's coming," Jenna giggled.

A moment later Jake spun my chair, placed his hands on my hips and lifted me. I wrapped my legs around his waist as my laughter escaped me.

"What are you doing?"

"Making it clear who you belong to." Jake carried me past the few tables to the bar. He set my ass on the counter and waved at Jeff. "I need a shot of whiskey, some salt, and a lime."

I caught Dillon looking my direction and I avoided his gaze. "We're doing a body shot, now?"

Jake's hands caressed my thighs then traveled up and around my ass and scooted me forward, closing the space between us. "Fuck yes, we're doing it now."

Jeff set the shot, salt shaker, and lime on the counter. "You better watch it, Jake. Nix is watching you."

That only ignited Jake's daring. With a smirk smearing his face, he winked at me. "Lay that sweet ass down on the counter."

I grabbed the lime and rolled my eyes at him before lying flat on my back. Jake sprinkled salt across my stomach, grabbed the shot, and swallowed. The tip of his tongue touched my stomach and with one slow, fluid motion, he gathered the salt, leaving behind a reminder of what that tongue could do. The lime left my lips, replaced with an immodest kiss. Jake's fist wound through my hair, his other hand tracing across my inner thigh, gripping me tightly while his lips devoured mine.

When he let me up for air, my face was flushed, my nipples hard against my shirt. I sat up on the counter, and he pulled my ass forward, closing his mouth over mine. Pulling my center against his hips, he pressed himself into me. My hands wrapped around his neck and held his face as his rough, passionate kiss continued. He pulled back from my lips with heavy lids and a hungry need in his eyes.

"I'm tempted to bend you over and take you here in front of everyone."

My eyes were set on him, but in my peripheral I could see we'd gathered the attention of the club members. "As tempting as that is, I don't want my brother to see that."

"I'm still gonna bend you over something." Jake tugged me against him, and I tightened my legs around him as he pulled me off the bar.

Jake lowered me onto the floor and took my hand in his. His eyes met Dillon's; I could see the animosity between them. Jake's stare didn't break until we passed him. Jake led me beyond several doors until we reached the courtroom. He pulled me in and shut the door behind us.

"Against the wall."

I put my back to it, watching him stalk toward me. He took hold of my wrist and turned me to face the wall. His heated breath blazed against my ear as his hands slid over mine. Pressing himself into my backside, he placed my hands on the wall above me, holding them with one hand.

His tongue slid over my ear, sending chills across my skin. The top button of my jeans came undone and his rough, calloused hand slid inside. He rubbed against my clit, pressing my underwear into me. A soft kiss on my neck was followed with an arousing bite, then another as he traveled down my neck and back up. Moving my underwear to the side, he slid into my wet folds. A hiss escaped his lips.

"Always so wet for me." With his circular motions and rhythmic flicks, he had my hips moving forward in an attempt to ride against his hand.

"You love it when I touch here, don't you, Peach?"

My breath left me when his fingers dipped inside and stroked me with ravenous force. My body tingled with a wave of arousal as his tongue slicked across my ear, sliding it between his teeth.

"I think you're ready for it."

His hands glided my jeans and underwear off my hips, easing each leg out. The touch of his fingers brushed along my skin as he slowly brought his hands up my legs.

"Spread them."

His hands touched between my thighs, spreading my legs wider. For a moment, I stood with my bottom bare, my hands against the wall, anxiously awaiting what pleasure would come next. When his mouth touched my center and his hands held my ass firmly in his hands, I knew what I'd been waiting for. Sitting below me, Jake glanced up with those wicked brown eyes before sliding his tongue in and out, penetrating me deep. A moan escaped me, my hips grinding against his greedy mouth.

CHAPTER TWENTY TWO

JAKE

THIRTY MINUTES LATER, the palm of my hand squeezed Peach's ass as we walked into the front room. Nearly everyone's attention was on us. My gaze met Dillon's first. With an acknowledging tip of his beer and a pissed off expression on his face, I knew it was clear to him who Peach belonged to. The corner of my mouth raised when Nix eyed me from across the room with his disapproving glare. I pulled Peach into my arm and claimed her mouth.

"I'm gonna play pool with the guys. Don't let any of my brothers touch you unless you want a fucking massacre in here."

Her vivid green eyes rolled. "I'll steer clear of Dillon."

As I slipped through the crowd, I looked over my shoulder to see Peach sitting down at the table with Jenna and a few other bikers' girls. Gripping a pool cue, I joined Nix, Trevor, and Max at the pool table.

Nix's arctic gaze raised to mine. "When I said claim her in front of everyone, that wasn't what I had in mind."

"Better get used to it." The back of my hand wiped the lips that were wrapped around Peach's pussy thirty-minutes ago. "She's my girl. I'll take her anywhere, anytime, whenever I damn well please."

Nix's jaw tensed. He set his pool stick against the table and with deliberate steps, moved to my side. He crossed his arms and leaned back. His cold, green eyes narrowed on mine.

"I'm gonna make myself real fucking clear. I'm not kicking your ass right now because I don't want to embarrass Liz, but if you disrespect my sister like that in this clubhouse again, I'll knock your fucking teeth out. She's not one of your floozies, but you just made her look like one tonight. I know every brother in here is wondering why I haven't murdered you, and we both know the two reasons I won't; my sister loves you, and you're the only one I trust to protect her."

My grip on the pool table tightened. My ego had just been thrashed, but I wasn't about to even the score when part of me knew he was right.

"I'll make damn sure everyone knows she means something to me."

"Good. You can start now."

"What?"

I turned to see what had caught Nix's attention. My stomach twisted when I saw who was standing by the door. Fiery red hair cascaded over slim shoulders and head to toe black fabric hugged every vivacious curve.

"You take Liz, I'll take Angela," Nix ordered.

My gaze swept between them. Peach had her eyes locked on Angela and was standing from her chair. Fists clenched, she was pushing her way through the crowd right toward her.

"Let that expression burn into your memory, Jake. That's Liz's *I'm going to fucking murder you* expression."

"I might have seen it a time or two."

Nix chuckled before navigating through the tables. Quickening my pace, I moved toward Peach and caught her in my arms.

"You look sexy as fuck when you're in a rage, but I don't want you hurt, Peach."

Standing on her toes, she peered over my shoulder. Her cheeks were flush and the adrenaline was clearly pumping through her jittery body.

"I can take her, Jake."

"I have no doubt you can, but we need to know why she's here." I glanced over my shoulder to see Nix pointing to his office. "She must have something to tell him." Brushing my thumb across her cheek, I attempted to soothe the wild cat within her. "Peach, stay here. I need to see what's going on."

"Jake."

My gaze hardened. "Peach, trust me. I need to be in Nix's office for this conversation."

"Fine." Her shoulders fell back and relief coursed through me.

I kissed her lips and quickly moved to catch up with Nix and Angela.

I opened the office door just before Nix closed it. He nodded to me, indicating his approval, then leaned against his desk, arms crossed. His stern gaze fell on Angela.

"You got some serious grit walking into our clubhouse."

"After everything that's gone on between us, I figured I owe you."

"Then let's hear it."

"Tolito wasn't willing to accept the majority of his crew ended up in jail by accident. He went after one of Otto's guys. They beat him to near death before he caved on Otto's deal. Tolito put the word out. He's looking for the anonymous buyer. Seven G's to the one who names them. If you know who the anonymous buyer is, you have the opportunity to collect seven grand, or it's time to put a plan in place to ensure Tolito doesn't find out who the buyer is."

Nix's eyes drifted to me momentarily, then returned to Angela. Tension tightened like a noose around my neck and spread to my chest. *Play it cool, Nix.*

"I'll put the word out. If we hear anything, I'll be sure to contact him."

Angela shifted on her heels. "If the buyer is someone you know, don't protect them, Nix. Tolito isn't one to fuck with. You know that."

"You back with Rex?" Angela turned to face me at the sound of my sharp voice.

"I appreciate what you did, Jake, but I can handle myself."

"You can lie to yourself all you want, but you know as well as I do, you're walking on thin ice. Men like Rex don't change. He'll keep beating you, and you'll continue to take it, until one of you is dead or in jail."

Her eyes softened as though she was having a moment of clarity, then it was gone, replaced with her usual calculated glare. "I gotta go. Think you can keep your sister off my back so I can get outta here?" She looked over her shoulder at Nix.

"Go out that way," Nix motioned toward the back door. "Everyone saw you come in and that'll raise enough questions."

Her hips swayed, giving us a show as she walked out. I turned my attention to Nix after shutting the door behind her.

"What the hell? Seven grand!"

Nix ran his hand through his hair. "Damn it! Stay with Liz. Everywhere she fucking goes, Jake. *Everywhere*."

"I will. What about giving Tolito a false lead?"

"No. We need to avoid being a part of it. We need to act like we don't know shit. Go get Pat. We need to tell him Tolito is hunting the people who put his crew in jail."

CHAPTER TWENTY THREE

LIZ

MY FINGER ENDED at the tip of the sparrow's wing on Jake's chest. I watched my hand rise and fall with each breath he took. Lying next to him on his bed, I moved closer to his body, and he held me tighter.

"What's wrong? You've been quiet since you're meeting with Nix and Angela. It still bothers me that you won't tell me what you talked about."

Jake's warm hand enclosed over mine, holding it against his chest. "Peach, I need you to trust me on this. It's safer for you that you don't know."

"I'm worried about you and Nix. I know about the deal."

"How?" Jake's grip tightened and he turned to me. "How do you know?"

"I overheard Nix and Pat talking about it."

"Son of a bitch." His head pressed against the pillow. "If you've listened in on his conversations, then someone else sure as hell could've too."

"You don't trust all your brothers?"

"No, I don't. I trust your brother, Trevor, and Max. Every man has their own self-interests and gaining seven grand is a hell of an incentive."

"Seven thousand for what?"

"Tolito is offering seven grand for anyone who gives him the name of who arranged the drug deal."

I sat up instantly as heartache and fear seized my chest. "No one can find out my brother set up the Royals!"

"Peach, listen to me." Jake's hands held my face as tears pooled in my eyes. "Even if Tolito finds out, it's him and only two or three of his crew. There's enough of us Kings to handle whatever comes our way, but *you* are the one who needs to be protected. You're the perfect tool for Tolito to use to get to Nix. I want you with me at all times until this business with Tolito is handled. I mean it, Peach. I want to know where you are every fucking minute of the day."

Jake's phone buzzed on the night stand and we turned our heads to see who was calling. Nix's number displayed on the screen. Jake instantly reached for it and answered. Worry crept into my chest, latching on, and causing a lump to grow in my throat.

"What is it?" Jake's tone revealed his concern. "Is he alive? Son of a bitch." His eyes widened and he held me in his fixed stare. "He knows. No, I'm not letting her out of my sight. You need to lay low. Don't go anywhere alone. I'll meet you there tomorrow."

Jake slammed his phone onto the night stand. "Damn it!"

"What's going on?" My heart pounded in my ears. "Is Nix okay?"

"Pat's house caught on fire sometime after he got home tonight. He didn't make it out."

My hand went to my mouth as tears streamed down my cheeks. Jake pulled me into his lap and pressed his lips against my head as he rubbed my back.

"Fuck, Peach, I'm so sorry. I know you grew up with him in your family."

"He was like an uncle to me." Through my quivering lip and sobs, I raised my head. "Did Tolito do this to him?"

"This wasn't an accident, but I'm damn sure they made it look like it. I'll find out more tomorrow."

"Jake, I'm scared for Nix."

Jake leaned back on the bed and laid me down with him. His lips gave a tender kiss to my forehead. "Don't worry about Nix. Tomorrow we'll make a plan to deal with Tolito."

"Can I come with you?"

"No, Peach. You're safe at the hospital. Nix and I have serious shit we need to deal with. I don't want you there for it. I want you as far away from this fucking mess as you can be."

My tears dripped onto his chest and his fingers wound through my hair, caressing my head. He turned me on my side and continued to run his hand over me, wiping my tears from my face, feathering kisses across my cheeks and forehead. He gently took hold of my hair and used it to bring my gaze to his. His bold, brown eyes had gone dark with emotion.

"There's nothing I won't do to protect you. Don't ever be scared *of anyone*."

CHAPTER TWENTY FOUR

———

JAKE

OPENING THE DOOR to Nix's office, it was obvious he'd barely had any sleep. I took the seat across from him. "You look like shit. Did you sleep at all?"

"No, I didn't." Nix raised his tired eyes from his desk. "I've been on the phone with local LE and TBI all morning. Pat's body was found and what was left of it will be autopsied. The investigator doesn't think it's an accident, but you know they can't confirm until they get the report back."

"We know damn well who did this. You said Otto and Pat were brothers back in the day. You think Tolito beating the hell out of one of Otto's club members made him start pointing fingers? You think Otto had an idea of who the anonymous buyer was?"

"He had to have. It's the only explanation I could come up with that made sense. And Tolito didn't just go after one of Otto's club members. I made some calls. It was Otto's nephew, Richard. He's in the hospital in critical condition. Otto loves Richard like his own son. Of course, Otto would've told Richard his own suspicions, and Tolito got what he needed out of Richard.

"There would've been only a few people who knew Otto's predicament. No doubt Otto shared it with Richard, and Tolito started on that short list. I know Pat wouldn't give up any information to Tolito, and the fucker murdered him for it." Nix's fist pounded the desk. "I want to take his ass out, Jake! Another good man had his life cut down by the hands of the Royals! Pat didn't deserve this!" Nix's eyes glistened with restrained tears. His voice lowered as he regained his composure.

"Where's my sister?"

"At the hospital. I dropped her off before comin' here. They have two cops working at all times. She's safe there. We both know Tolito wouldn't go after her there."

"How'd she take the news?"

"She cried for a while and couldn't fall asleep. She's scared something might happen to you. I made her drink some whiskey, so she could sleep."

"I should be the one looking after her." Worry etched deeper into his current frown lines. "I owe you."

"You don't owe me shit. I love her. She belongs with me. She's just as much my responsibility now as she is yours."

"I still owe you. Under all that asshole, you're a good man."

"I know you're hurtin', but don't get all sentimental and shit."

Nix chuckled. It was good to see his eyes lighten from the heavy weight of his stress. That only lasted a few seconds before his thoughts changed and he spoke again.

"I need you to call in all the Kings. We need to tell them what's happened to Pat."

"When you tell them, we need to watch their reactions." I stood and pulled my phone from my pocket. "There's a chance someone's been listening in on your conversations and knew about the deal. Tolito may have found out from them and not through Richard. Peach said she overheard you talkin', and I did too. That means another member could've overheard and seven grand is plenty enough incentive to turn on a brother."

Nix ran his hand through his hair and his eyes scanned the desk in thought before meeting my gaze. "Call 'em in."

Every Kings member sat at the courtroom table awaiting what Nix had to say. As he explained Pat's death, I watched the reactions of every one of them. Only two gave me concern; the new prospect, William, and Lucas. Lucas' eyes shot down to the table and his cheeks burned red. William showed no emotion at all. His lack of emotion was reasonable being a new member of the club, not having that bond yet. Either way, both of their behaviors were odd, putting them on my radar.

"You think Tolito did this?" Max asked. His large stature leaned back in his chair. The dark ink rolling up his neck flexed with his tense muscles.

Nix's tired eyes met Max's. "I do. Tolito's crew was arrested Tuesday night for the illegal possession of drugs, guns, and several other charges. Tolito thinks his crew was set up and is on a manhunt. I believe someone pointed their finger at Pat and Tolito took matters into his own hands."

"Why the hell would Pat's name be mentioned?" Trevor asked, his tone sharp.

Nix uncomfortably glanced at me before returning his attention to Trevor. "Otto Macari participated in a drug deal with the Wild Royals before Tolito's crew was arrested. Pat and Otto ran in the same club back in the day. Pat was a connection. A connection I believe Tolito tested."

"What do the cops think?" Wesley pressed.

"They're doing an autopsy. When the report comes back, they'll have more answers."

Dillon leaned forward, setting his elbows on the table. "So, we don't know if Tolito really did have anything to do with the fire?"

Nix let out a breath. "No, I don't have any proof. It's a hunch."

"Do we need to be worried? Is Tolito going to come after anyone else?" William asked nervously.

"If he went after someone it'd be me," Nix ran his hand through his hair, his nerves and exhaustion were getting the best of him, "but I want all of you to be on alert and don't ride anywhere alone until we know more."

Axel, the slick baldy with the spider web tattoo etched across his neck and shoulder, cocked his head. "When's the funeral?"

Nix's lips twisted, clearly trying to control his emotions. "Depending on when his body is released, but I'm planning for Sunday. We'll do a ride in his memory and come back here to the clubhouse for dinner after the service. I want everyone in their colors for the ride."

The members drifted into heated discussions, and I nudged Nix by the arm, drawing him away from the group.

"Did you notice any unusual behavior?"

Nix's gaze swept over the group. "Our prospect William, and Lucas seemed on edge."

"Same here."

Nix shifted the weight of his boots. "I'm not going to question the loyalty of any member with unjustified suspicion. Every one of those men are loyal unless proven otherwise."

"When they leave, we need to talk."

Nix and I rejoined the others. Questions were already being raised about member safety and who would replace Pat's position. Nix took the time to reassure every member and explained the support we would be receiving from the TBI. By the time the meeting was adjourned Max had announced he'd campaign for the VP position. Several members agreed his qualifications would benefit the Kings.

After another hour, the group scattered, leaving only Nix and me. I followed his heavy, laden steps to his office. His head raised when I walked in.

"What do we need to talk about?"

"We're going farther down this shit hole and there's things you need to know before it gets deeper."

Nix folded his arms and leaned back on his heels. "Let's hear it then."

"There's a reason I've never shared my past with you or any other brother."

"I don't know how much more shit I can take right now." Nix pulled out his chair and sat with a weighted thud. "You sure this is a good time to come clean about somethin'?"

"It's best you know, so we can move forward." I pulled out the chair across from him. I was about to bring up old memories, not something I enjoyed doing. I rubbed the back of my head, then met his fixed stare.

"Before moving to Nashville, I ran with an outlaw crew. They were dangerous, unpredictable criminals. Same as the Royals, but I didn't join them voluntarily. I was an undercover agent. I was in deep and witnessed a buddy of mine, a good friend, get murdered by his own brothers. Brothers I thought were loyal to one another, but missing money led to distrust, distrust led to suspicion, and there was no room for suspicion in the Silent Skulls. After his death, I burned my colors and left. I left everything behind. The job, the year I'd invested collecting evidence. Everything. I turned in my badge and went in search of a fresh start. I couldn't do it anymore. Being a part of that gang changed me. I didn't give a shit about anything and was drifting through life, trying to figure out where the hell I belonged." I leaned forward on my elbows, gauging his reaction. His steady gaze awaited me to continue.

"You offered for me to prospect, and I saw potential for a life here, but I still didn't give a fuck about much of anything until Peach. Being the Kings' President, you have to look at the big picture; the safety of your sister, the club members, the shop and bar, but I don't. The only thing I give a damn about is keeping her safe. I understand you don't want to believe any of the Kings would be capable of selling you out, but we both know men are capable of doing far worse for very little. You need to assume every member is a potential rat. We need to start asking the right kind of questions. Seven grand is enough motive for any one of them to turn on you."

"An undercover, huh?" Nix's eyes narrowed as he stared at the desk then slowly raised to mine. "This explains a lot of shit about you. The Silent Skulls, I've heard of them. They have a hell of a reputation. It's best you got out when you did before you were in too deep."

"They demanded loyalty, and I was beginning to feel my undercover work was betraying them, but seeing your friend gutted and his body burned can do things to a man. I knew I had to get out, or I never would. Not alive, anyway. I'm telling you this because we need to assume all possibilities. Don't put it past any of the members to cut a deal with Tolito for the money. It's best you tell Jenna to stay away for a while, and I promise you, Peach won't be leaving my sight."

With a tilt of his head and silent thoughts, he rubbed his fingers across the unshaved stubble on his chin. "Telling me about your past; I'm sure it's not easy. I respect that and I'm hearing what you're saying. After tonight, I'm gonna tell Jenna to avoid my house and clubhouse for a while. She's not gonna like it, but she'll deal. I'm not telling anyone else this, but you; I'm moving into the clubhouse. It's safer here with the in and out traffic. Last thing I need is to wake up to a knife or gun in my face."

"That's smart. I'll bring Peach by tonight to pick up more of her things."

Nix nodded, his sullen eyes were hiding deeper emotions than he was revealing. "Tell her I'm sorry. My mistake is putting us all at risk. You don't know how much she means to me. She's all I have left. I trust you not to let anything happen to her."

"I'd kill a man before I'd let him hurt her."

"I believe you."

CHAPTER TWENTY FIVE

———

LIZ

I STOOD IN my closet, gathering more clothes to load in my duffle bag. Jake stood in the doorway of my room with his giant arms folded, a watchful gaze on me.

"I like this."

"You like what?" I asked over my shoulder.

"You packing to stay with me."

"I'm already staying with you."

Heavy steps padded across the floor. His warm, masculine presence invaded my space, strong arms wrapping around my stomach as his front formed to my back.

"You know we'll be making a trip back here to get everything of yours, don't you?"

"I do." Wet lips trailed along my neck, sending little shocks of pleasure down over my arms.

"You want that? To stay with me, for good?"

"Yes."

Lifting my shirt with his thumb, he ran his fingers across my belly and slowly traveled into my shorts. "There's somewhere I haven't had you yet."

Slow strokes rubbed over my underwear, wetting me beneath, as his low, sensual voice filled my ear.

"I want you on your bed, spread bare for me."

My underwear was flicked aside and with one quick thrust, two fingers filled me. Jake turned my head and caught my breath with his mouth. His lips dominated mine with carnal need. Pleasure swam through me in waves as his fingers caressed and stroked and thrust again. His hand left my neck and wrapped around my waist. I was lifted with one arm and his other left me to take hold of my ass.

My backside hit the mattress and he stared down at me. His gaze radiated dominance and desire. His hand waved in the air.

"All of it… off."

Sitting up, I slowly removed my shirt. His eyes fell to my breasts and waited for me to unclasp my bra. When the fabric fell to the floor, his tongue ran across his lips. He removed his shirt and unbuttoned his jeans. As he folded them down, I could see the hard bulge in his briefs.

"Your shorts," his command snapped me from my trance.

Unzipped and unbuttoned, I slid them off my hips and hooked my fingers into my panties, removing my last piece of clothing.

His hand reached inside his jeans, taking hold of himself. Pulling out his erection, he stroked it repeatedly. My eyes fell to his hand moving over the length of his erection as wanton need burned between my legs.

"You want this cock, Peach?"

"Yes."

"Work for it." His hands spread my knees and I laid back on the mattress. Rough fingers grazed across my opening. "I want to watch you." His fingers left me and took hold of my hand and placed it where his had been. "Show me how much you want it."

He stepped back and took hold of his shaft, stroking it in his fist as I rubbed along my opening. Sliding one finger in, I slowly ran my finger across my clit. His gaze remained on me, his eyes glistening with hunger, continuing his firm strokes. My head tilted back as pleasure seized my body. Taking my breast in my hand, I kneaded it while moans and gasps escaped my lips.

"Fuck, Peach, tell me you want my cock in you." His pumping grew feverish as my moans grew louder and my strokes harder.

"I want it, Jake. I want you to fuck me."

"Damn, I need this pussy."

Strong hands took hold of my thighs and pushed them down, spreading my legs wide for him. With one quick motion, he took hold of his erection and plunged into me. My walls clenched around him as his heavy lids fell and his head tipped back. With each hard thrust, my ass cheeks smacked against him. With relentless need, he pounded into me, drawing my orgasm to its crest.

"That's it, Peach. Come for me. Soak my fucking cock."

My hands fisted the comforter as my body trembled and a wave of release shot through me. Pulling out, then plunging back into me, he gave one hard thrust, and his head sunk back as a growl escaped his chest.

His grip on my thighs eased, and he lowered himself onto me. I wrapped my legs around him as he ran his hand through my hair, settling it on the nape of my neck. Soft kisses were brushed across my chest, up my neck, and finished on my lips.

"There's nothing better than being inside you." Another kiss met my lips. "I love you."

"I love you too."

Laughter escaped me when he buried his face in my neck and licked and nipped at my skin. His head raised and a smile split his lips.

"You better fucking love me."

After getting dressed, Jake helped me finish packing and as he loaded my bags into my car, Nix pulled up in the drive. My relief and eagerness to see him couldn't be contained. I fell into his arms and he patted my hair.

"I'm sorry, Liz, for everything."

I could hear the emotion in his voice. He lifted his sunglasses into his hair and I saw the self-condemnation in his eyes.

"This isn't your fault, Nix. You and Pat made a choice together. He knew what you were getting into with this deal, and he chose to do it anyway. It was worth the risk to him."

"I was hesitant to do the deal. I never should've agreed. Now everyone is at risk."

"Pat wouldn't have given Tolito any information, you know that. Tolito has nothing on you."

Nix's gaze met Jake's. Silent words were exchanged before his gaze returned to me. "I hope he didn't, but seven grand is enough incentive to cause any man to do something stupid."

"Not any man." I shook my head as Jake's arm wrapped around me. "Neither of you would, and I don't believe any of the Kings would either."

Nix let out a sigh. "You always see the good in everyone, it's a fault we both share."

Jake kissed my head before nodding to Nix. "Get what you need. We'll leave together."

Thirty-minutes later, Jake and I left in my Camaro, and Nix left to see Jenna. We stopped by the grocery store before heading home. Jake took Rocky out to play before helping me unload everything into the house. While he and Rocky snuggled on the couch and watched TV, I prepared dinner.

"What are you makin' in there? It smells good."

"Chicken Alfredo."

Jake's hands slid around my waist as I stirred the noodles. His chin rested on my shoulder as his hand grazed along the top of my shorts.

"You in my kitchen, cookin' in these little shorts, is making me stiff."

"You'll have to keep it reined in, playboy. Dinner is ready."

"Then I'll have you for dessert." A wave of pleasure rushed through me as he nibbled my ear. His palm squeezed my ass before reaching over me to the cabinet, grabbing and setting two plates on the counter to be filled with pasta.

"This is damn good, Peach." Jake's hand rubbed along my leg as we ate. "What have we been eatin' out for when you could've been cookin' for me?"

"You really like it?" A smile smeared my face.

"Hell yeah."

The rumble of motorcycles stopped Jake mid-bite. He set down his fork and headed toward the front door, his shoulders tense. "Rocky. Here." Jake pointed to his side and Rocky came immediately.

Jake looked out the side window as the rumbling of the engines stopped outside the house. A crash exploded through Jake's front window, spreading shards of glass across the furniture and carpet. I jumped off the stool and ran to Jake.

His hand took hold of me. "Go into the hallway and get down!"

After sprinting across the room, I put my back to the wall and slid down to my feet.

Jake moved into the kitchen and lowered a fake drawer. Taped to the inside was a .40 caliber. He pulled it from the tape and headed to the front door. The rumbling of motorcycles echoed through the broken window. I could hear voices outside, growing louder as they approached. The sound of glass crunching under the weight of Jake's boots was followed by the cocking of his pistol.

"My gun is loaded and pointed right at you. Don't take another fucking step."

Rocky growled and then a gunshot boomed through the house. My body clenched from the loud boom. The voices shouted at one another, then faded into the distance, the sound of their engines dying out as they hurried down the road.

Jake turned the corner, pulled me into his arms, and kissed my head. "We need to go, now. Grab your things as quickly as you can."

"Jake, what's going on?"

"They were Royals, here to settle the score for Rex or on Tolito's orders. We're gonna stay at the clubhouse. Pack your things."

Grabbing only the most important essentials, I rushed to fill my bags and followed Jake with a load to the car. As soon as his bike was in sight, we saw the tires had been slashed.

"Son of a bitch." Jake's jaw tightened and he shoved the bags into the Camaro. After pushing his Harley into the garage, he closed it and went back in for Rocky and his kennel.

I dialed Nix as Jake drove us to the clubhouse. "What's going on?" Nix asked, his voice strained.

"Wild Royals came to Jake's house. They threw a brick through his window and slashed his bike tires. He had to shoot off a warning shot to get them to leave. We're headed to the clubhouse to stay the night there."

"You all right?"

"Yeah, shaken up, but fine."

"I'll be at the clubhouse in thirty-minutes."

Jake and I finished carrying our bags to one of the offices turned living quarters and settled Rocky into his kennel. We went downstairs as soon as we heard movement. Jake pushed me against the wall, keeping his hand on me as he crept along the hallway, his gun raised and ready to fire. Nix called out to us and Jake lowered his gun. We turned the corner and Nix and Jenna greeted us. Nix hugged me tight, stroking his hand over my hair.

"You sure you're all right?" His tired eyes searched my face, reading my emotions.

"I'm fine. I promise."

Jenna hugged me next and squeezed me in her long arms. "Why were the Royals at your house?" she asked Jake.

"I'll take first watch," Jake nodded to Nix. "You need sleep."

"C'mon, babe," Nix took Jenna's hand, "he's right."

Jenna kissed my cheek, turning to follow Nix upstairs.

Jake leaned against a table, pulling me between his legs. He set the gun on the table and wrapped his arms around me. "You need sleep too. You gotta work tomorrow."

"I'm not leaving you."

Jake's jaw tensed as if he wanted to argue, then his grip tightened, and he pulled me in for a kiss. "Bring the blankets and pillows down."

My makeshift bed made the hard floor bearable, but no matter how uncomfortable I was, I wasn't leaving Jake's side. He tucked the blanket over my shoulder and held me firmly against him.

"Do you think it was Rex or Tolito who sent the Royals to your house tonight?"

"Both." Jake's fingers stroked my hair. "I think Tolito knows the Kings are involved with the deal somehow and taking me out would be two birds with one stone. No doubt they want to fuck me up for what I did to Rex and the other guy."

"Jake, I'm scared of what's going to happen. What they did to Pat, I'm still struggling with it. The fact that he's never going to walk back in the clubhouse. I've lost so many of my family already. I can't handle it if anything happens to you or Nix."

"Don't be scared, *ever*." Jake's lips pressed against my forehead. "Everything will be fine. Nix and I will handle it. Try to get some sleep. You have work tomorrow."

Repeated strokes of his fingers through my hair soothed the tension in my body. My heavy lids and the comfort of his touch forced me into sleep.

CHAPTER TWENTY SIX

LIZ

THREE DAYS LATER, after Jake fixed his window and replaced his tires, all the Kings members and their girlfriends awaited the signal to begin the memorial ride in Pat's honor. It was a warm day, the sun blasting heat over my skin. I adjusted the shades over my eyes and settled my feet on the foot pegs. Jake rubbed along my leg and glanced back at me.

"You good?"

Placing my hands around his waist, I nodded. "Yeah."

His hand squeezed my leg, then he fired up the engine. Axel, the Kings' Road Captain, started first, then each bike moved forward to follow. Nix and Jenna took off behind Axel, then us and the rest of the crew.

Cutting through the breeze on the warm day made the ride enjoyable given the circumstances of the ride. We all needed this though. The last few days had been rough. Everyone was on edge, wondering if Tolito and his crew would come after anyone else. Nix and

Jake told the crew the Royals were likely after Jake for what he did to Rex and the other guy who attacked me, and we had no reason, so far, to believe otherwise. Nix explained Rex had beat up Angela and that alone was enough justification for Jake's actions.

The memorial ride ended at the funeral home where Pat's service was taking place. His remains had been cremated and given to Pat's sister, Louise. Nix had helped her arrange the funeral and even paid for some of it.

As the warm sun sent sweat trickling down my back, a sullen feeling rested in the pit of my stomach. I was dreading our arrival at the funeral home. Pat was the third man in my life who had been ripped away from this world, and my fear of what Tolito was doing behind the scenes plagued me each day. We still didn't know if Tolito knew more about the deal than we thought.

Nix and Jake had become cautious around the rest of the Kings members. Not enough for them to notice, but I did. Their conversations were kept private, away from the others, and they seemed to have a watchful eye on each member and their activities. Jake was on high-alert, keeping me with him at all times, and he and Nix continued to take turns staying up at night at the clubhouse.

Axel was the first to pull into the funeral home and each of us lined up along the parking lot next to him. Pat and Louise's family and friends welcomed us as we entered. Jake held me tight and kissed my head before we took a seat.

Tears poured down my cheeks as Nix and others took turns speaking about Pat and the good memories they had of him. Jake's fingers wound in my hair and he pulled me against him. His gentle kiss pressed against my temple.

"It's okay, Peach. Let it out." His hand rubbed along my thigh as the other strummed through my hair.

When the service ended, Nix and Louise stood by the exit, listening to condolences and thanked everyone for attending. Axel led the Kings and funeral attendees back to the clubhouse for an early dinner. Jake and I stayed behind, waiting while Nix took care of final details with the funeral home. The staff began removing chairs and roses, and I stood in the archway staring at Pat's silver urn. Jake wrapped his arms around me and rested his chin on my shoulder.

"You okay?"

"This is our home, and we're living our lives watching over our shoulders. It's not right. It's not right what they did to him. I want them gone."

Jake kissed my neck and cheek. "Leave these things to me. None of this is your problem."

"But it is." I turned in his arms. "I worry about you both every day and now Jenna is involved. She's Nix's girl, that puts her at risk, too."

Jake held my face in his hands. "It's only a matter of time before Tolito fucks up and makes a mistake that gets his ass killed or in jail. In the meantime, let me take care of things. It's my job to carry the burden, not yours." His hand took hold of mine. "Nix is finished. You ready?"

I glanced over my shoulder to see Louise pick up Pat's urn. My attention returned to Jake with tears stinging my eyes. "Yeah."

Jake and I followed Nix and Jenna out. As I raised my leg over the passenger seat of Jake's Harley, I noticed three motorcycles parked on the other side of the street, Royal colors visible on the vests, their gazes locked on us as we mounted our bikes. I tapped Jake's arm as tension coiled in my gut.

"Do you see them?"

"I see them."

"What are they doing here?"

"It's a warning. They want us to know they're watching us."

Jake pulled back his vest, revealing the Glock strapped inside, then fired up the engine. The three riders pulled out onto the street and rode off.

Nix's gaze fell on Jake. "He knows."

"They just made that pretty fucking clear."

We arrived at the clubhouse and the food Nix had catered in was already being served. We got in the buffet line, then joined the others at the tables.

Aunt May nudged me and smiled before leaning in for only me to hear. "How you doin', doll?"

"You know it's hard seeing another family member taken."

Her arm rubbed along my back. "I hear Tolito might be responsible."

"Nix doesn't have any proof, but I know he's right."

A pained expression filled her face. "Of course, he's right."

Nix pulled his buzzing phone from his pocket and left us to go to his office. Jake stood and followed. Several members watched them leave.

"What's that about?" Lucas asked, sounding worried.

I shrugged. "I'm the wrong person to ask."

I tapped Jenna's shoulder. "I'm going to the bathroom."

She nodded and went back to her conversation with Crystal.

When I walked out of the bathroom, Dillon was leaning against the wall waiting for me.

"Where's Jake?" I asked him.

"Still in the office with Nix."

I attempted to move past him and he blocked me. "You really wanna be with a guy like him?"

"You obviously don't know him well or you wouldn't be asking me that."

"I know him well enough to see how he treats you, like you're another one of his fuck toys."

"Are you serious right now?" My arms crossed and my hips shifted my weight. "That's not how he treats me."

"From my point of view, it is. You deserve someone better than Jake."

"I'm guessing you mean you."

"Me or someone else. Anyone, but that asshole."

"He may be an asshole to you, but he's incredible to me." I shoved past Dillon and moved down the hall. I stopped and turned to him. "And don't let Jake catch you cornering me like that again. Not if you want to keep those good looks."

Returning to the front room, I grabbed my plate and tossed it. I'd lost my appetite and needed air. I placed my hands on Jenna's shoulders.

"I'm going outside."

"I'll come with you."

We walked out the front door and the evening breeze hit me, shedding some of the tension from my shoulders. I leaned against the wall and glanced at the setting sun, making its descent into the orange and pink sky.

"What's wrong?" Jenna asked.

"Dillon had the nerve to corner me in the hall and tell me I deserved better than Jake. He's an asshole. He doesn't know shit about Jake. If he did, he wouldn't be saying that."

"Why let something that idiot said bother you?"

"It's everything; Pat's death, the threat Tolito's men made today, the brick through the window. I'm on edge every day, constantly worrying when the next strike will happen and how bad it's going to be."

"I'm really worried about them too." Jenna gnawed her lip and joined me against the wall. "Nix isn't sleeping well. He's really worried about everyone. You in particular. He's thankful for Jake. With how protective he is of you; it's taken some of the pressure off Nix."

My head lifted to the sound of Harleys coming down the road.

"We have some late arrivals."

I waved at the guys on the bikes and cocked my head at the lack of colors. "I don't recognize them."

I moved away from the wall to get a better look. Their bikes pulled alongside the street, but they didn't cut the engines—two men, one bald and burly with a dice tattoo on his neck. The other biker with dark, thick hair, and a handsome face nodded his head at me.

"Nix around?"

"He's inside." I motioned my thumb over my shoulder. "You can park here and come in."

The man's arm reached out and took hold of mine, gripping it painfully. "Get on the bike."

"Let go!"

A squeal came from Jenna and I turned my head to see the dark-haired man had left his bike and was now covering her mouth while his other arm clutched her against him. Giant arms wrapped around me, lifting me in the air. I kicked my legs out and struck the dark-haired man in the face. His grip loosened on Jenna.

"Run Jenna! Get Jake!"

Hands and arms squeezed me hard, forcing me onto the bike as Jenna ran inside. My hand was shoved into cuffs and locked onto the metal bar behind the passenger seat. My heart pounded in my ears as I kicked and thrashed at them. A fist slammed into my face and jolted my body. I slumped against the bald man's back as the sights and sounds around me drifted away.

CHAPTER TWENTY SEVEN

JAKE

"What did the TBI say?"

Nix set his phone on the desk and leaned back in his chair. "It's been declared a homicide. They'll be calling each of us in for questioning. They're looking into the Royals too."

"You needed proof and now you got it. Tolito's responsible, you know it. The threats are escalating. He knows more than we thought. We have a rat."

"You're right." Nix let out a breath. "Pat never would've given Tolito information. Tolito is getting it from someone else."

"Jake! Jake!"

At the sound of Jenna screaming, I stepped to the door and swung it open. Jenna came barreling in, followed by Dillon.

My chest tightened. "Where's Peach?"

"They took her." Jenna's eyes were wide with fear. "Two men on motorcycles. One had a dice tattoo on his neck. The other had dark hair and a tattoo across his hand. We were outside when they drove up and tried to take us both. Liz kicked the guy who had hold of me and he loosened his grip enough I got away."

"Fuck." Dillon raked his hand through his hair. "They weren't supposed to take her."

My body moved across the floor in seconds. My fists grabbed his vest and slammed Dillon against the wall.

"Where the fuck did they take her?"

"I don't know."

"Why would you help that son of a bitch? He's gonna hurt her!"

"He wanted to take you out. She was never part of the deal."

I pulled Dillon forward and slammed him back into the wall. His head cracked against it and his hand went to the back of his head.

"You stupid mother fucker! You turned on your own brothers for a measly seven grand and now Tolito has Liz! What? All because I took what you thought was yours. She was always mine!"

I released my grip and swung. My fist contacted his face and the rage inside me unleashed. Another swing and blood spattered from his lip.

"I didn't collect the seven grand," Dillon spat out.

"What do you mean?" I pulled my bloody fist back from his face.

"I don't know anything about the drug deal! Tolito and his crew cornered me. They wanted to take you out for what you did to Rex and Tony."

My eyes narrowed on his. "What did you get in return?"

"My own life. It was me or you. I gave them your address. That's it. I wasn't willing to die for you and I knew you could handle yourself. You had a better chance than I did."

The sound of Nix racking a shotgun pulled me from my interrogation.

Jenna sucked in a breath.

"We'll deal with him later." Nix nodded toward the door. "We need to move. Get Max and Trevor."

Jenna latched onto Nix. "Maybe you should call the police."

I shook my head as rage coursed through my veins. "We don't have time for the police. It won't be long before Tolito beats and rapes her. We need to get to her as fast as we can."

"Where do you think he took her?" Jenna squeaked out.

My gaze shifted to Nix. "She's gotta be at his clubhouse. It's manned with his remaining crew, private, and already set up for his needs."

Nix called the Kings into the courtroom. His heated stare narrowed in on each member. "Tolito took Liz. We need riders. We're going after her. We're riding armed, so if anyone says no, I understand."

Max nodded. "I'm in."

Trevor tapped his vest. "Same here."

Axel stepped forward. "In."

Wesley shook his head. "I can't boys. I'm getting too old for this. I'll stay behind and deal with things here."

Nix nodded and focused his gaze on Lucas and William. "What about you two?"

William shook his head. "Nah man. I'm not gonna ride hot."

Lucas' hands trembled and his body twitched uncomfortably.

I stepped toward him. "Fuck, Lucas, you on something?"

"This has gotten outta hand," Lucas murmured.

I grabbed his collar and spun him toward me. "What do you mean? Start talking. Now!"

"I was in deep, Jake. I owed Tolito thousands."

"What is it? Coke? Heroin?"

"Cocaine."

"Did you sell out Pat?"

Tears filled Lucas' eyes.

"You son of a bitch. You sold him out for the money!"

"I'd overheard him on the phone one night. Then Tolito offered the money. I had my girl, Crystal, tell 'em what I'd heard. He gave her the money and I paid it back to him." His voice cracked. "I never expected him to go after Liz. I'm sorry, man. I just needed out before he came for me. He'd already sent a couple of his guys after me once."

My body shook with rage.

"Jake, please, man, we'll get her back."

I slammed Lucas onto the table and swung. Blood spattered across the wood. "After he fucking rapes her and let's his brothers do the same?"

"Stop him before he kills the bastard!" Trevor shouted.

Another swing landed then several arms dragged me from Lucas' limp body.

"He's out cold," Wesley said, standing over Lucas.

Nix grabbed my arm and met my gaze. "Got your shit together?"

I rubbed my swollen, bloody knuckles and nodded.

"Then we need to fucking go. We're wasting time."

CHAPTER TWENTY EIGHT

LIZ

THE PAIN IN my face shocked me when I woke and moved my stiff jaw. As I moved, the handcuff rattled against the frame of the bed I'd been put on. My eyes surveyed the room. It was bare, other than the bed, a night stand, and a large mirror on the wall with a clear view of the bed. I looked at my reflection. My cheek was red and swollen. There was no pain anywhere else on my body and I let out a breath of relief; I hadn't been raped.

The door opened and I swallowed the lump in my throat as the dark-haired man I'd kicked in the face walked into the room. He closed the door and approached the bed. His dark eyes studied me head to toe. His tongue ran across his bottom lip before he sat on the edge of the bed. I pulled away from his touch when his hand grazed my leg.

"Gorgeous and feisty. No wonder your brother sent you away. I wouldn't want a man like me anywhere near my sister either." Putting his hands on both sides of me, he moved toward me, crawling over me on the bed. The scent of his cologne and sweat churned my stomach. I shimmied away from him, and he gripped my leg, pulling me under him.

With my free hand, I swung at his face. "Don't touch me!"

He caught my hand mid-air and squeezed it in his grip until the pain made me grimace. He released my hand and moved closer. "I'm gonna touch you, darlin'. I'm gonna touch you everywhere I damn well please. Then I'm gonna stick my cock in you and fuck you over and over." His hand crawled up my inner thigh until he reached between my legs. "When I'm done with you, I'm gonna let every one of my brothers have their chance to fuck you."

I shoved his hand away as the vomit rose in my throat and fear clenched my gut. "Why are you doing this?"

"Your brother got involved in things he shouldn't have. Now I need to teach him a lesson. Would you rather me kill him? I can do that. I can save you the pain…" A wicked laugh escaped him, "Well there'd still be pain. I can't let a pretty thing like you go without knowing what this pussy feels like around my cock, but I'd keep my brothers off you. Do you want that instead?"

I held my lips tight. I wasn't going to be baited into his fucked-up mind games.

He moved in closer and brushed his lips against my ear. "You're a smart girl, aren't you?"

I kicked out, making contact with his waist, knocking him off the bed. He landed and quickly rebounded.

His palm slapped across my face. "Not smart enough!"

My hand went to my throbbing cheek. With teeth clenched, I glared at him. I knew Jake would come and this bastard would pay for everything he did to me.

"Dominic, bring me more handcuffs!" His dark eyes lowered on me. "You could've made this easier on yourself. I wouldn't have hurt you as badly if you'd given in willingly."

"There's no way in hell I'd give in to having sex with you."

The tall, burly man with the dice tattoo on his neck walked in and when his eyes fell on me, my nerves bunched into a tighter knot. He handed the man I assumed to be Tolito the second set of cuffs.

"Leave something for us, boss."

"It isn't gonna be tonight." The corner of Tolito's mouth raised. "I'll be busy with her all night long."

The burly man chuckled and walked out; my stomach churned at Tolito's words. This would be over soon. It had to be over soon.

Tolito bent over the bed and reached for my hand. I pulled it away and his hand slapped across the opposite cheek, rocking me backward.

"Give me your damn hand." He lunged for it and gripped it in his fist. His free hand took hold of my hip and with one quick, forceful motion, he flipped me over and raised my ass in the air. The cold, heavy handcuff clasped around my wrist and dragged me forward to the bed frame. It locked in place and Tolito ran his hand along my arm. I cringed at his touch and tried to move away from his body. He instantly seized me in his grip.

"You have too many clothes on. I want to see what I'm working with."

The tearing of my shirt sounded in my ears and cool air hit my bare back. With his fists gripping the fabric, he removed my shirt completely and tossed it onto the floor. His hands reached around me and cupped my breasts, squeezing them. Teeth scraped along the skin of my back, then a hard bite came down, pinching my skin, making me wince in pain.

"Stop touching me, you sick fuck!"

"Oh, darlin', we're just beginning." His hand slid over my backside and reached between my legs and stroked. I clenched my legs shut and wiggled away from him. The cuffs clanged against the bars, and he took hold of my hips, jerking me back in place. His fist took hold of my hair, yanked my head back, and his tongue licked across my cheek.

"Give me what I want and I promise I won't kill your brother."

I grimaced at the tight, painful hold he had on my hair. Anger surged through me as I spit out the words. "I don't trust a damn word you say."

Tolito laughed into my ear. "You're right, you shouldn't. I'm gonna kill him anyway, but I want him to see what I do to you first."

Tolito shoved me forward, then his weight left the bed. As soon as the door closed behind him, I instantly tested the bars and searched for a weak spot. Rust had gathered at one of the joints. I jerked hard on the bar and continued to try to jolt it free. The door started to open and I stopped immediately.

Tolito placed the camera he held on the night stand and pressed the red record button. He climbed back onto the bed and gripped my hips hard, moving them where he wanted them. His hands came around my waist and unbuttoned my jeans. I bucked and writhed, trying to break free from his grasp. His fist came down on my back, forcing me to collapse onto the mattress. Tears pooled in my eyes as the pain rippled over my muscles.

"I told you once already, this will go easier if you cooperate."

CHAPTER TWENTY NINE

LIZ

MY BACK ACHED from Tolito's punch and was tender to his hand running across my skin. Forcefully grabbing my hips, he lifted my ass into the air. Terror rushed through my body when his hands took hold of my jeans and jerked them off my hips. His hand slammed down on my ass cheek and jolted me forward. My body began trembling at what was to come if Jake or Nix didn't make it in time.

"I bet you like it rough, don't you, darlin'."

A hard, pain inflicting smack came down on the same cheek. I bit into my lip and grimaced, refusing to make a sound and give him any satisfaction. Another hard smack hit the opposite cheek, then another, jolting me forward with each swing, bringing tears to my eyes.

Relief filled me when his weight left the bed and his painful smacks ended. I glanced over my shoulder and the knot in my stomach constricted when I saw him undressing. Hidden tattoos traveled down the left side of him and into the briefs he was pulling down.

His erection sprung forward, and I looked away as tears rolled down my cheeks. *Please Jake, hurry.*

His weight returned to the bed, and I instantly brought my legs forward, stopping him from taking my jeans off any further. Strong hands fisted my ankles and dragged them out from under me. Quick, aggressive movements had my jeans sliding off my legs. Another slap to my ass was followed by an excruciating bite to my tender flesh. My hair was fisted and yanked, arching my back and bringing my face to his as he pressed his erection into my backside.

"Hell, I might just keep you as my ol' lady if you're as good at fucking as you are at taking a beating." His bite came down hard on my shoulder as he hooked his hand onto my thong and tugged it off my hips.

The distant sound of gunshots instantly loosened his grip on my hair. "What the fuck?" He jumped off the bed and rushed to get his jeans. The door swung open behind me and Jake charged in with his gun raised. One look at me and his eyes darkened. His gaze fell on Tolito and he fired. Tolito's body slammed into the wall as the bullet tore through him. Blood poured out of his abdomen and onto his jeans. Another round was fired and Tolito's body collapsed to the floor in a twisted heap. Gurgles choked out of his mouth before he exhaled his last breath.

Tears streamed down my cheeks and I let out the breath I'd been holding.

"Jake," I cried.

"Peach, baby," Jake came to the bedside and stroked my hair, "let me find the key."

He searched Tolito's clothes, returned to the bedside and stroked my head before unlocking each cuff. Gripping me in his arms, he held me tight against him. My tears soaked into his shirt. Soft strokes ran through my hair and over my back.

"Ssh, Peach, it's okay. I'm here. I got you." I raised my head, and his hand caressed my cheek, wiping the tears from my face. Fear filled his eyes as he looked down at me.

"Did he rape you?"

I shook my head. "You stopped him before he did."

Jake pulled me back against him and kissed my head. Cradling me in his arms, he lifted me from the bed. My eyes caught sight of Tolito's dead body and the blood pooling on the floor.

"Peach, don't look at him."

I buried my face into his chest. He set me down on the other side of the bed and grabbed my jeans. As I put them on, he removed his vest and shirt. Raising the shirt, he nodded for me to put it on. I slipped into it, then reached for the camera.

"He was recording what he was doing to me." I pulled the SD card from the camera and handed it to Jake.

"Sick son of a bitch." Jake glanced at Tolito's body, then back at me. He pocketed the camera card. "Come here. I need to get you home." Jake pulled me into his arms and hugged me tight. His hand stroked through my hair as he kissed my head. "Tolito made the biggest fucking mistake of his life trying to take you from me."

"Thank you for coming for me." My tears wet his chest as my adrenaline and emotions came crashing down.

"Always. I'd do anything to protect you."

Jake took my hand and gently led me out of the room. Down the hall lay another body. Jake covered my eyes and guided me to the stairs. Nix was waiting at the bottom of the steps with a gunshot wound to his arm. I rushed to him, and he held me tight against him, patting my hair.

"You all right? Did he hurt you?"

"Not like that. Jake stopped him."

Nix's chest loosened. His grip eased and I looked up at him. His eyes glistened with tears. "Jake's gonna take you home. I need to call TBI and get patched up. I'll come by Jake's house later."

"What about the bodies?" Panic rose in my chest. "What's going to happen when TBI comes?"

Jake wrapped an arm around me and kissed my head. He and Nix exchanged silent words as they looked at one another.

"Everything is going to be fine," Nix assured me.

CHAPTER THIRTY

———

LIZ

JAKE PROPPED ME up on the bar, a wicked grin shining across his face. It'd been three weeks since Tolito kidnapped me and everything was finally calming down for the Kings. Lucas' colors were stripped from him and he was given a beating that put him in the hospital. I stopped in his room one evening after finding his name on the chart. Part of me sympathized for the bruises on his body, but it was his actions that got Pat murdered and me assaulted. I could forgive him, but I'd never forget.

Jake came clean about his past as an undercover, and it was his connections that kept him and Nix from landing in jail, along with the edited video of what Tolito did to me. TBI's investigation determined that Nix and Jake shot in self-defense and charges were never pressed.

I glanced down at Jake as he spoke loud enough for all the club members to hear.

"This woman here," he placed his hand on my waist, "is the best damn thing that has ever happened to me, and I want every one of you fuckers to know, I love her."

Hoots and hollers shouted throughout the clubhouse. Jake came between my legs and wrapped his hands around my face and buried his fingers in my hair as he claimed my lips. My breath grew heavy as arousal burned between my legs. Jake hadn't touched me intimately since my assault, determined to ensure I was healed and wanted him, and more than anything, I wanted him now. His head met mine. I bit my lip and grinned.

"Take me upstairs."

Jake's eyes lit up and he instantly pulled me from the bar. My legs wrapped around him as he carried me through the front room, completely oblivious to everyone watching.

He laid me beneath him and gently ran his hands along my stomach as his lips found mine. Sliding beneath my jeans, he eased two fingers inside me. My breath left me the moment his touch filled me. My body was aching to have him thrusting into me, but I wanted to savor every moment of his touch.

Kisses trailed along my neck as I arched my head and moved my hips, giving him better access to my clit. His hand slid out and unbuttoned my jeans. I raised my hips as he slid them off and tossed them aside. Slowly his hand traced along my tattoo then lowered, diving into my panties and filling me, stroking deep, settling into rhythmic swirls around my clit.

"Tell me what you want, Peach. I'll do it to you."

"I want you to make me come, Jake. Make love to me, then fuck me like there's no tomorrow."

ACKNOWLEDGEMENT

Thank you to Jackie V. Booknerd for your inspiration of
Castle of Kings. Without your photograph challenge, readers
wouldn't of had the opportunity to meet
Jake Fucking Castle.
To book nerds everywhere;
you are my tribe
you make my dream possible
and for that
I thank you.

OTHER BOOKS BY BETTY SHREFFLER:

FIRE ON THE FARM
(A Second Chance Cowboy Romance)
Losing the man she loved to a terrible accident, pushes Amy Flanders into a life of independence. Her only source of comfort is her work—a business dedicated to the care and training of horses. Until one lonely night leads her into the arms of Brock Baisdin. A man who fulfills her deepest desires and reignites a flame long forgotten.

Between his picky tastes and running his own business, Brock Baisdin has little time for women, but that doesn't stop him from looking for love. After saving Amy from a cancelled date, Brock is instantly drawn to the shy and beautiful woman hiding secrets beneath her lust-filled baby blues—secrets he finds himself eager to discover.

Undeniable attraction pulls them into each other's arms. Hope draws them into each other's lives. For Amy Flanders, Brock Baisdin may be the man to bring love back into her lonely life, if only she can overcome the wounds of her past and face her biggest fear—risking the pain of another shattered heart.

MY HOT BOSS

Emma

From the moment I met Grayson Cole, I knew he was someone I wanted to let in my panties and maybe, even in my heart. One night, one sexy-as-sin kiss, and several drinks later; our incredible evening turns into a disaster. I never thought I'd see him again after that, no matter how many nights I spent wishing I would. Until a month later, he waltzes into my office as—MY NEW, HOT BOSS. I'm so screwed.

Grayson

She was meant to be a fun fuck. That's all I wanted. That's all I needed. But Emma Williams could never be just that for me. The quirky, brunette vixen challenges me at every opportunity. My desire to have her has me working for her affections, like I've never done before. What is this woman doing to me? Not only am I her Boss, but I don't do feelings. There's only one way I see this ending. I'm fucked for sure.

WHEN HUNTER MEETS SEEKER

(An Arcane Society Novel)

Trained by the Arcane Society to fulfill her legacy as an Arcane Hunter, Anya Carlisle knows nothing but the loneliness that comes with being a hunter. One evening, in a place she never should've been, throws Anya into the heated snare of Dex Grigori. She should've seen him as the enemy, but instead her body longs for his touch in ways she's never experienced.

From the first moment Dex sets eyes on Anya, he wants her all for himself. After one night of forbidden passion he's left craving more of her, until he discovers how wrong for him she is. She's a deadly hunter that kills without question and he's exactly the kind of demon she's been trained to eliminate. Yet his fierce desire to have her brings him dangerously close to her heart, where he soon discovers she is far more than the cold killer he anticipated.

EMBRACE THE DAWNING

(Book 1, The Covenant Series) Kayci Pierce possesses strength, endurance, and accelerated healing that set her apart from normal humans—traits she's never understood and kept hidden since childhood. She feels disconnected from the seemingly normal world around her—until she's attacked by a creature she didn't know exists and then rescued by a stranger she can't forget. Dreams of the attractive, dangerous man haunt her and lead her into a world she was born for.

Adrian Spade spends most of his solitary nights hunting rogue vampires for the Covenant, until an undeniable attraction leads him to reveal his vampire identity and risk his life by saving Kayci's. Tempted by her mysterious nature, Adrian finds himself drawn to Kayci and becomes her protector while she discovers her heritage and what it means to be a half-breed vampire sorceress.

Kayci's relationship with Adrian brings her as much passion as it does danger. Now with a vampire revolution beginning and a romantic connection to a full-blood vampire, Kayci must work with Adrian to survive surrounding threats. As Kayci tries to make sense of an unfamiliar world, she's forced to choose between the life she's always known and her vampire birthright.

CRUEL TEMPTATION

(The Covenant Series, Book 2)

The war is over. The rogue vampires dispatched. As a full-blood vampire and sorceress, Kayci Pierce finally feels safe. Her focus now set on how to run the Covenant and best protect her species. The next-in-line, Lycan clan leader shares Kayci's vision—but his captivating and sexy brother, Cassius McCabe is a distraction Kayci can't afford.

New threats surround Kayci as she navigates unfamiliar territory and feelings she can't hide. Will temptations destroy her and everything she's worked for, or will love be enough to pull her back from the edge?

DARK AND BEAUTIFUL NIGHTS

(The Covenant Series, Book 3)

One man will fight to keep her love while the other will do whatever it takes to win it.

Devotion keeps Kayci longing for Adrian's return. Dark magic is the only way to free him and its cruel seduction has captured Kayci in its embrace. Cassius, unwilling to lose the one thing he's longed for—his mate, fights for Kayci's heart and saves her from her biggest threat...herself.

Pulled between unrestrainable desire for Cassius and her devotion to Adrian, leaves Kayci suffering from the worst battle she's ever encountered...the one for her heart.

ABOUT THE AUTHOR:

 Betty Shreffler is a bestselling author of paranormal romantic suspense and contemporary romance. She writes sexy and suspenseful stories with hot alphas and kickass heroines that have twists you don't expect. She also writes beautiful and sexy romances with tough women and their journeys at finding love. Betty is a mix of country, nerdy, sassy, sweet and a whole lot of sense of humor. She's a fan of photography, reading, watching movies, hiking, traveling, drinking wine, bubble baths and all things romantic. She lives with her amazing hubs and five fur babies; two rescue pups and three cats. If she's not writing or doing book events, then you can find her behind the lens of a camera, in the woods, or sipping wine behind a deliciously steamy book.

Ways to stay in touch with Betty:

AUTHORBETTYSHREFFLER

GROUPS/AUTHORBETTYSHREFFLER

BETTYSHREFFLER

@BETTY_SHREFFLER

@BETTY_SHREFFLER

WWW.BETTYSHREFFLER.WORDPRESS.COM

Made in the USA
Columbia, SC
08 July 2018